"Is something wrong?" Blake asked.

He parked in Abby's semicircle driveway, leaving his headlights to shine over the front porch.

"I don't think so." She forced a smile and searched in her bag for the house key. But a feeling of dread passed through her. Something *was* wrong.

Likely it was nothing more than nerves—hardly surprising after the day she'd had. "I guess the sensors on my porch lights are broken. Those lights usually come on when it gets dark."

"Let me come up to the door with you, just to be safe. You weren't too steady on your feet earlier, and shouldn't be stumbling around in the dark." He turned off the engine, but left his headlights on to shine over the front porch.

Blake stood back as she went in and reached for the lights. Nothing happened as she flicked the light switch.

"Looks like the power is out."

Blake's hand came down on her shoulder, giving her a chill.

"Shhh," he whispered. "There's someone else in the house."

Books by Kit Wilkinson

Love Inspired Suspense

Protector's Honor
Sabotage
Plain Secrets
Lancaster County Target

Love Inspired

Mom in the Making

KIT WILKINSON

is a former Ph.D. student who once wrote discussions on the medieval feminine voice. She now prefers weaving stories of romance and redemption. Her first inspirational manuscript won the prestigious RWA Golden Heart. You can visit Kit at www.kitwilkinson.com or write to her at write@kitwilkinson.com.

LANCASTER COUNTY TARGET

KIT WILKINSON

HARLEQUIN® LOVE INSPIRED® SUSPENSE

Recycling programs
for this product may
not exist in your area.

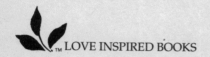 LOVE INSPIRED BOOKS

ISBN-13: 978-0-373-44593-6

LANCASTER COUNTY TARGET

Copyright © 2014 by Kit Wilkinson

www.Harlequin.com

Printed in U.S.A.

Whatever your hand finds to do,
do it with all your might
—*Ecclesiastes* 9:10

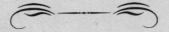

To my lovely student, Emily Dingman,
what a pleasure to watch you mature into such a
fine young lady over the past three years.
Tu rends le monde si mieux—You make the world
better. Always remember you make a difference.

ONE

What is that doctor doing in here?

Abigail Miller's heart beat fast and hard as she stood, frozen, in the dark hospital corridor, watching a surgeon empty a large syringe of clear liquid into a patient's IV drip.

Why? What is he doing here? Alone with a patient in a closed-off part of the hospital?

Abby shook her head. It didn't make any sense.

Dressed in full scrubs with no ID badge that she could spot, the doctor's figure towered over the male patient who lay lifeless on the gurney. As large as the surgeon looked in the narrow corridor, the male patient looked small even on the hospital gurney—his olive skin pale, his head round and bald. He seemed so still.

Abby sucked in a quick breath and decided to backtrack without disturbing the doctor and patient. She wasn't comfortable confronting the tall, imposing surgeon herself, but something about the scene just didn't seem right. Perhaps she could find a security guard… She stepped backward and her shoe squeaked as it turned on the tiled floor.

"How did you get in here? This part of the hospital is closed." The doctor spun toward her, his voice booming through the empty hallway. His cold, gray eyes flashed in the dim emergency lighting and chilled her like an arctic blast. The rest of him was hidden beneath a complete workup of surgical scrubs, including face mask, gloves and hat.

"I was just cutting through here. I do it almost every day." Abby forced her lips to move while her eyes stayed fixed on the surgeon. "I was on my way to Maternity. I hope that's not a problem."

"I don't understand how you got into this area." He advanced toward her, forcing her to take several steps back. "The entrances are supposed to be locked. This patient is highly contagious. This area is under restrictions. You shouldn't be here."

Contagious? Abby hadn't heard about any restrictions. Surely there would have been signs, announcements. The sense of something wrong grew stronger. Pulse rising, she skirted to the side of the large man and looked down at the patient's chart attached to the end of the gurney.

N. K. Hancock—TRANSFER.

In the dim lighting, that was all she could read, but she could see that the papers were solid white. If the patient were contagious, the chart would be marked with a prominent red stripe. Abby swallowed hard. Her heart drummed against her ribs. This doctor was lying—if he even was a doctor. She needed to find a security guard, stat. But first, she had to get away. She composed herself just enough to keep from sinking under the doctor's menacing glare and looming figure.

"I'm sorry, Dr...." Abby waited but he did not supply a name. With each syllable, she inched herself away from the man and his patient. "I didn't know we couldn't pass through. Again, I'm sorry to disturb you, Doctor. I'll just be on my way." She turned and headed for the stairwell.

"Oh, no, you don't." He was behind her in seconds. Over her. Around her like a giant spider. He grabbed the top of her arm and squeezed her flesh like a vise. His cold eyes flickered in the dim lighting.

She trembled and fought against him, but her struggles were in vain as the grip of his stubby, sausagelike fingertips dug deeper and deeper into her skin. He pulled her tight against his stout belly. She had no hope of breaking free.

Was this her just deserts after finally deciding she would not join the Amish church, defying the wishes of her father?

She'd gone to school to become a nurse, but she hadn't made her final decision about living the Plain life until recently. It had been time to put away one or the other and stop living on the fence. So last week, she'd laid aside her prayer *Kapp* and her frocks for good. She'd devote her life to nursing, delivering babies and helping others to stay healthy. But the choice had not come without a lot of pain, especially to her father, the *Ordnung* bishop.

Her father's words still rang through her head—a verse from the Psalms. *"If you stand in the counsel of the wicked, you will become wicked."*

Had she made the worst decision of her life? Right now, it certainly seemed that way. Tears filled Abby's eyes. Crazy, desperate thoughts swirled around in her mind. She continued to try to break free of the doctor's grip, but she could not come close to matching his strength. Her breathing came in short gasps. She would have yelled but there was no one to hear her.

"You've been exposed." The doctor's tone mocked her

as he dragged her across the hallway. "I'll have to give you an injection, too."

"What?" *Is he mad?* "Please, stop. You're hurting me. Let me go."

With his free hand, he produced another full syringe from the pocket of his scrubs. The needle shook as it came at her. His fingers closed in tighter around her arm as he yanked her sleeve high, exposing the skin above his grip. The hot prick of the needle stabbed her and the drug burned like fire as it entered her bloodstream. "What? What did you just give me?"

The doctor yanked her to the end of the corridor and through the door to the stairwell, not seeming to care that he crashed the door frame's metal edge into Abby's forehead. The blow radiated across her skull. Nausea waved through her gut as the drug made her head light—too light. Her body began to collapse. She could feel her blood pressure fall…

Please, Lord, help me.

Finally, she felt his fingers release her. She slumped to the cold, tiled floor.

The empty stairwell spun around her. The strange doctor had vanished. With all her might, she tried to reach for her cell phone. It was in her back pocket. But the drug was hitting her full force now. Her hand shook uncontrollably and the device dropped from her fingers. Her eyelids closed as she groped the floor desperately for the phone. But it was no use. She was going under and there was nothing she could do to stop it.

Please, Lord…help…

Abby closed her eyes and the darkness overtook her.

"Code Blue. Code Blue. Paging Dr. Jamison. Room 307. Code Blue. Dr. Blake Jamison."

The announcement blared through the overhead speakers. Everyone in the operatory stopped what they were doing and looked at Blake.

Code Blue? How could there be a Code Blue? It signaled that one of his patients needed resuscitation, but that couldn't be true. He had taken on exactly three patients since transferring to Fairview Hospital. They'd been recovering well, awake, alert and resting as of two hours ago. This had to be a mistake.

"And clip." He opened his gloved hand and waited for the nurse to place the suturing instrument in his palm. With a delicate touch, he closed up the tiny incision, returned the instrument to the nurse and removed himself from the operating area. The surgical staff would have to finish the cleanup after his first surgery at Fairfield Hospital of Lancaster County, Pennsylvania. Apparently, he had an emergency to look into.

"This way, Doctor." One of the nurses tugged at his sleeve, guiding him toward the doors. "Take the service elevator. It's faster. I'll show you."

A minute later, Blake entered a patient-recovery room where a crash team had assembled with a defibrillator. An unresponsive male patient, mid-to-late fifties, lay on the hospital bed. He was not one of the three patients Blake had seen earlier. Blake turned to the young nurse working near the monitors. "I'm Dr. Jamison. I was paged for a Code Blue, but this man is not my patient."

"Cardiac arrest," she said. "Started about fifteen minutes ago. Heart stopped soon after."

"But he's not my patient. I can't treat him. Hospital policy. It could lead to a lawsuit and an insurance nightmare."

She glanced back at the chart and pointed. "Your name is the only one on the chart."

"That's not possible."

She stared back at him with a go-ahead-and-look face.

Blake picked up the chart and thumbed through the pages. Unfortunately, the nurse was correct. His name was there. And what certainly looked like his signature. "I'm telling you this is a mistake. I've never seen this chart before. I've never seen this patient before. What kind of operation do you run here at Fairview?"

"This is no joke, Doctor. This man is in cardiac arrest and that chart says you're his doctor. I'm just the floor nurse. I have nothing to do with doctor assignments."

Blake stepped up to the bedside, opposite the working crash team, and put aside the chart. The nurse was right. He was wasting his breath getting upset with her. He'd have to speak to the appropriate people at the appropriate time—after he had done everything he could to treat the patient. "What's the history in a nutshell?"

"A nutshell is all we have," the nurse continued. "We have no idea. He came in this morning. A transfer patient from New York City. Some sort of insurance issue? Apparently, he's recovering from laparoscopic cholecystectomy."

New York City? The place Blake had just escaped? Or tried to, at least.

He shook the spiraling thoughts of his parents' devastating plane crash out of his head. Today another man's life was on the line. He was a doctor. For the moment, that was all that really mattered. Forget insurance headaches. Forget his own personal grief and struggles to sort out his life.

"You're saying this man had gallstone surgery somewhere else, was brought here and is now in cardiac arrest?"

She nodded.

"What medication has he been given? Does he have any known allergies?"

"I don't know. As you saw for yourself, there's not much in the chart and he only arrived an hour ago," the nurse said. "We can't seem to revive him. Hospital policy is to give it fifteen minutes. Should we call?"

"Not yet. Draw blood," Blake said. "I want a basic workup. And while we are waiting, continue efforts. I want to know more about what's going on."

The nurse took blood samples and scampered out of the room. The crash team continued to work.

"Stand by," one of the crew said. The other member prepared the electric plates to try to restart the patient's heart. "Three, two, one."

The man's body popped from the voltage. The monitor beeped once before the flatline signal returned. Wait and repeat. Blake glanced through the chart. He was still certain he'd never seen this paperwork before or the patient who went with it—Nicolas Hancock. The name was not familiar. But on the last page, there it was—*Dr. Blake Jamison*. With a likeness of his signature.

Clearly, someone had made a very big mistake and Blake intended to find out who was responsible.

After a few minutes, the nurse returned with the basic blood screen. She handed the report to him almost breathless.

He read over the graphs and figures. Adrenaline levels were off the charts. That would certainly cause someone to go into cardiac arrest. "Any idea why his adrenaline would be so high?"

"No, sir."

Blake looked up at the IV drip. "Did you attach this?"

"No, sir. He arrived with the IV in place. But I did replace the fluids."

Blake tried to think of a scenario where a patient would have so much adrenaline in his body. The only explanation that came to mind was that he'd received a dose of epinephrine—a drug which could not be tested for, since the body already made it naturally. But a dose large enough to cause this sort of reaction was anything but natural.

This man's cardiac arrest was looking as if it had been induced. Blake shook his head. Something very strange was going on here, but there was one thing that was certain—Mr. Nicolas Hancock was dead.

"It's time to call," he said. "Time of death is twelve-oh-seven."

The nurse wrote down the hour.

"Is there a next of kin?" Blake would hardly know what to say to them.

"No, sir," the nurse answered, her tone softening a touch. "His file says to contact his lawyer in case of an emergency. I'll be glad to do that for you."

"Thank you." Blake rubbed his chin, deep in thought. This was not what he'd signed up for. He'd come to Lancaster County hoping for some peace to get past the loss of his parents, and to figure out what to do with the sudden discovery that he'd been adopted as a baby.

But he could hardly think with all this unorthodox nonsense at the hospital. If this had been an accident of some sort, then someone had really fouled up, medically speaking, with this patient. Blake wanted to know who and why. "I'm not signing a death certificate until I get some more information on this patient. This situation is—" Blake could not keep the strain of emotion from his voice "—unacceptable—medically, ethically and professionally unacceptable. Get the hospital administrator down here. Someone needs to look into this."

The nurse began to shut down the machines. "I'll inform Dr. Dodd."

Blake headed toward the door. He felt a dark cloud over him. The same one he'd had over him in NYC. He stopped in the doorway and turned back to the nurse. "So you changed the drip bag. But did you change the IV tubing?"

She shook her head. "No. The tubing was securely in place. I didn't see any reason to insert another IV needle into the patient."

"Then save the entire IV, tubing and all, in a hermetically sealed container. It's possible medications or a mixture of medications were administered prior to his arrival that caused the cardiac arrest. We have to cover ourselves legally in this day and time. Also, I'd like a copy of that chart. I want to find out how my name became associated with this patient."

"Of course, Doctor. Naturally."

Naturally? There was nothing natural about any of this. This was the twenty-first century. You didn't lose patients to gallstone surgery.

"Dr. Blake Jamison. Dr. Blake Jamison, please report to the E.R. as soon as possible. Please report to the E.R."

No way. This is not happening. Blake let out a deep sigh as he stepped back into the elevator. *At least it's not a Code Blue.*

"This way, Doctor. Follow me." Janice, a nurse assigned to assist him in the E.R. just the day before, held a grim expression. She led him to bay ten, where she stopped and flipped back a flimsy blue curtain.

"She's one of our nurses…Abigail Miller." Janice pulled him inside.

"I don't know her." Blake shook his head. A face that beautiful he definitely would have remembered. He drew closer. She was early twenties, pale with a long, golden braid flung across her shoulder. Her forehead had a nasty contusion. Her left arm sported a rough and fresh abrasion. "What happened to her?"

Janice shrugged. "The custodian found her like this

in the stairwell off the third floor. Out cold. She hasn't even blinked."

"Pulse?"

"Rapid. BP low. This was found next to her." She handed him a large syringe.

Epinephrine, he read on the side label. Blake handed the syringe back to the nurse. With his other hand, he felt the woman's racing pulse at her neck. Her breathing was labored. Traumatic stress? "Get her on a monitor. Are you sure she was injected?"

Janice shook her head. "It was beside her. That's all I know."

"Is she known to have any severe allergies?"

Janice shook her head again. "No. She's never sick. Healthiest person I've ever met."

"You're sure nothing's broken? You moved her?"

This time Janice nodded. "Yes, Doctor. I'm sure the orderlies were very careful. No one would want to hurt Abigail."

Blake touched her cold cheek. "Miss Miller? Miss Miller? Wake up. I need you to tell me what happened."

On the outside, she lay there like Sleeping Beauty. On the inside, Blake knew that her body was fighting for its life. Janice rolled up the mobile heart monitor and began to put the sensors in place. As the cold nodes stuck to her skin, Abigail awoke with a start. She sat up, gasped for air and tried to reach for Janice. "It hurts. My chest. It hurts. I can't bre—"

The heart monitor sensors reacted with an alert.

Blake kept a firm hand on the woman's shoulder, pushing her back down to the bed. "Prep me a dose of Inderal, stat," he said. "She's going into cardiac arrest."

Just like Nicolas Hancock.

TWO

Streams of blinding white light seeped under Abigail's heavy eyelids. Beeps and buzzes echoed in her ears. Everything around her whirled in a blurred circle. Fatigue. Nausea. Pain. Everywhere pain. Especially her head.

"Ugh." She lifted a sore arm only to touch a nice hard knot on the front of her head. *Ouch. What in the world? Where am I?*

She glanced around the small space. Heart monitor. Oxygen supply. Blood-pressure gauge. Blue hospital curtain wrapped around the small bed she lay in. *I'm in the Emergency Room!*

"Hello." A tall, sandy-haired man peered around the curtain at her, then stepped inside. He wore a white lab coat over a pressed blue oxford. His stethoscope and Fairview ID badge hung loosely around his opened collar.

"How are you feeling, Abigail?"

"I'm feeling a little confused." She looked down at her limp body in the hospital bed. "I don't remember how I got here.... I don't know you, Doctor, do I?"

"Nope. I'm new. Jamison. Blake Jamison."

"Nice to meet you, Dr. Jamison." Her mouth was dry and it hurt to try to sit up.

"Call me Blake. Please." He smiled. "And take it easy.

You've had a pretty rough day. Don't worry if you aren't remembering everything just yet. You will."

Her head was foggy and thick, but she tried to focus. An IV drip fed into her left hand. The doctor—Blake— sat on a stool to her right. She was suddenly very aware of the fact that he was a handsome man, with a nice build and a kind face.

"So, why am I here?"

"I was sort of hoping you could tell me that. Maybe once your head clears up." He took her wrist in his hand. He studied her face as he counted her pulse. A strange and awkward sensation passed over Abby as his fingertips pressed her skin. She was unaccustomed to the touch of a man and especially that of a fancy *Englischer*.

"I didn't know Fairview was getting a new E.R. doctor. When did you start?"

"Well…I'm just here temporarily. I'm filling in for Dr. Finley."

"Oh, right. I remember now reading something about him teaching a course in one of the hospital newsletters. I didn't realize he would be away from the hospital for that. Do you often fill in for doctors on leave?"

"This is my first time. I have a private practice in New York. I'm just here for a change of scenery. Eight weeks. Then I'll go back." He released her arm. His lips pursed, as if he was thinking about something far away. "Seventy- two. Much better. You had me pretty scared there. Never a dull moment at this place."

He used his stethoscope and listened to her breathing and her heart. Then he whipped the instrument out from his ears and again rested it like an adornment around his neck. The light scent of musky cologne wafted over her.

"Did you say *never a dull moment?*" She tilted her head

and glanced at him sideways. "I am still at Fairview Hospital, right?"

He chuckled and started to respond when an electronic device at his waist began to vibrate. "See what I mean?"

He took the phone into his hands, silenced it, read the message and returned it to his waist. "Not important. So, how's the head?"

"It's a little tender."

"I'll have Janice bring you some Tylenol. Drink lots of fluids. Get some more rest. I'll check back in another hour."

"Wait. I have questions. You can't leave yet." She wanted more information than that. "How did I get here? Where did this bruising come from? Why am I hooked up to a heart monitor? How long was I unconscious? And why?"

His phone began to buzz again. He clenched his jaw as he looked at the screen and silenced it. "Sorry. Friends back in New York who think I'm available 24/7. Not important. Again. And that's a lot of questions. I thought the doctor always asked the questions."

"You can't expect me to just lie here and not know what happened." She met his steady gaze.

"I might if I think that's what's best for you."

What? Who did this doctor think he was? Was he really not going to tell her anything? "At least tell me what day it is."

"It's Thursday," he said, following it up with the date.

"Thursday," she repeated. She leaned back into her pillow with a frown. It seemed that her memory was only missing most of one day. The damage could have been much worse...and yet it was troubling to think of those lost hours, especially given the injuries she'd sustained.

"You look upset." He stepped back inside the curtained

area. "Worrying about your memory may only block it longer. Try to relax. Think about the things you did early this morning."

Abby shook her head. "Nothing. I don't remember a thing. Please, isn't there anything you can tell me about what happened? At least explain the heart monitor."

"Well, we aren't completely certain, but apparently, you took a hefty dose of epinephrine." His words were slow. His tone kind and compassionate. "Fortunately, you're strong and your body quickly absorbed much of the excess. We gave you something to calm your heart. It worked just the way it was supposed to—the monitor is just here as a precaution. You're going to be fine. There will be no long-term effects."

"Epinephrine?"

"Yes, it almost threw you into cardiac arrest."

"How? Why would I take epinephrine? That's crazy. Are you sure?" In a blink, Abby had a flash image of a shaking hand raising a needle to her arm. It was dark, like nighttime.

"You were found with an empty syringe, which we are pretty certain contained a killer amount of epinephrine before having a meeting with your arm."

"Wait a minute, what else? I—I..." She looked down at her bruised arm. Her pulse started to rise. Someone had held her. So tight. She remembered her arm had felt as if it might break. She also remembered a man so close she could feel his breath on her neck. Abby shivered. "Someone gave me a shot. He was holding me around the arm. But where was I? And how did I get here?"

Blake's lips pressed together as he seemed to consider how much to tell her. He frowned. "The custodian found you on the third floor. He said you were out cold in the stairwell by that big hall that's being renovated. He's the one who brought you down. He saved your life. Now, look, you're getting too worked up. Try to rest. We can continue this conversation in a bit. You're very weak."

The third floor. Cold gray eyes. Abby could feel the tension rising in her, and it wasn't because of her condition. She locked eyes with the doctor. More images shot through her mind. *Gurney. Syringe. Eyes. Icy, fiery eyes.* She flung the sheet off her lap and swung her legs over the side of the bed. "I need to go back upstairs. Someone's in trouble. I wasn't the only one who was injected."

Blake placed a hand on her shoulder that gently but firmly kept her from moving. "Slow down, Abby. You could still be under the effects of the drugs."

"No. Really, I'm fine." She slipped from his reach and stood. Her legs felt like cooked spaghetti. Blake caught her as she leaned back for support.

"It will have to wait, Abby. You need to rest."

"I'll rest later." She pushed the doctor and his restraining arms away.

She didn't remember all the details of her attack, but she knew someone else had been in danger. She couldn't wait a minute longer—she might already be too late.

Blake could hardly believe the beautiful but provoking patient had talked him into letting her out of bed. Of course, when she'd plucked the IV from the back of her hand with a single yank, it was clear she was going to get up to the third floor with or without his approval. Since his shift had ended, he thought it best to accompany her. At least that way he could confine her to a wheelchair and keep an eye on her.

"Janice told me that you were raised Amish," Blake commented as he wheeled her into the elevator.

She nodded. "It's true."

"So why did you decide to stop being Amish? If you don't mind me asking?"

She laughed. "I don't mind you asking at all. But I wouldn't say that I stopped being Amish. I may not wear the clothes, but in here—" she touched her chest where her heart would be "—I will always be Amish. I didn't take vows to commit myself to the church because I wanted to continue nursing."

The elevator stopped at the third floor and Blake turned them toward the renovation area, taking in her words, which were more personal to him than she knew. "At the risk of sounding ignorant, I'm going to ask. Nursing isn't allowed?"

"No, it's not. It's *Hochmut*." Abby smiled and waved hellos to the few staff members they passed. "The Amish can have shops, build furniture or buildings, and farm. Professions that require higher degrees are not pursued."

"Hochmut?"

"Ja. Hochmut," she repeated with a teasing look, correcting his pronunciation.

"I don't speak Pennsylvania Dutch." Blake felt himself blush—her unfamiliar words were just another reminder of how little he knew of this place where he had come to find answers about himself.

"It means 'arrogance.' It's what comes with letting the world in, with studying and learning more than needed. By going to school and becoming a nurse, I've become too much a part of the world. In many ways, I'm not worthy to take vows. But I have vowed in my own way to take care of people. My people. They need health care that they are comfortable with and I can provide that. I think I made the right decision. One day my family will understand. Some of them already do."

Blake tried to wrap his head around the Amish culture.

After the letter his mother had left him, he'd researched anything and everything Amish. But now that he was there in Lancaster, he realized there was still so much to learn. And there was already one strike against him. Would his biological family think less of him for his medical profession?

"How about you?" She looked back at him with her bright blue eyes. "Why did you leave New York? And how did you pick Fairview Hospital of all places?"

Blake had a stock answer for that question. It was the one he'd given to everyone else who'd asked him, even his closest friends. No one knew the real reason he'd come to Lancaster. He'd told no one that he had recently found out that he'd been adopted, that he'd been born in Lancaster, not in New York City as he'd thought his entire life. He could hardly process the news himself, much less deliver it to others and expect them to understand. It was best to sort it out first. By himself. Yet he found himself on the verge of telling Abby the truth.

"Lots of reasons," he said in a low voice.

"Dr. Jamison. Dr. Jamison." The young nurse from Nicolas Hancock's room raced after him, waving a set of papers. "Here, Doctor. I called Mr. Hancock's lawyer, but I only spoke with a receptionist. She wouldn't let me through, nor would she tell me if there was a next of kin to notify."

"Thank you." Blake took the papers.

She glanced at the closed doors to the renovation area and easily guessed their intentions. "The renovation area has been locked up after what happened to you, Abby. But if you want to take a look, then we might have a key at the station." She started back in the direction she'd come. "I have your hermetically sealed IV and tubing, too, Doctor. Would you like to have that, too?"

"Yes, if you could bring the IV, too, I'd appreciate it."

Abby looked up at him. "Hancock? Did she say your patient's name was Hancock?"

"Yes. Nicolas Hancock." He handed Abby the chart so he could steer the wheelchair. "But he wasn't really my patient. Supposedly, he was a transfer. Somehow my name got on that chart. My signature, even—but I never laid eyes on him until I was paged for a Code Blue. I came right away but it was too late. The crash team tried and tried to resuscitate but he didn't make it."

Abigail stared down at the front page of the chart in her lap. "I've seen this before."

"Seen what?" Blake thought again about the fact that Hancock and Abby had had elevated adrenaline levels. Had that not been a coincidence?

"This chart. This name. This patient." Her eyes were wide.

"What? What do you mean? I thought you worked in Maternity."

Before she could answer, the young nurse returned with a set of keys to unlock the refinished wing. She opened the doors and handed Blake a small sealed plastic bag, which had *Hancock* printed across the side. He hung it on the back of the chair, thanked the nurse for her help and rolled Abby into the closed-off wing. The farther they got into the hallway, the more the blood had drained from Abby's face. He stopped the chair and walked in front of her. He took her arm and checked her pulse.

"Your heart is racing and you look really tired, Abby. This is too much. Let's go back down and rest. As you can see, the hallway is empty. There's no one else here."

"That doctor was *here*." Abby, white as snow, pushed him aside. She stood and began to move through the dim hallway. "He was here. In this hallway with that patient."

She pointed at the chart. "He gave him an injection. Blake, I saw it. I wasn't supposed to, but I did. That's why he injected me, too."

"What doctor? What are you talking about?" Blake moved quickly around the wheelchair and put a hand under her shoulder to support her. He took the chart from her hands and tossed it back onto the wheelchair so he could take her hand. "I really think this is too much for you right now. Please sit back down. You're not really making a lot of sense."

"He tried to tell me that patient had a highly contagious disease, but I knew it wasn't true. There was no indication of it on his chart." Her pulse quickened as she pressed against him.

Blake didn't answer. She was already too worked up. He should never have let her talk him into this stupid excursion. "You need to be resting. Come on."

Abby continued, ignoring his efforts to make her return to the wheelchair. Her persistence was admirable, he supposed. But as a doctor, he had to object to the way she was putting herself at risk. But she would not stop. She continued down the hallway without his help.

"So how did he die?" She looked back at him.

"Cardiac arrest."

"Too much epinephrine?"

"Too much adrenaline. Yeah. Probably epinephrine. We saved the IV tubing—that's what's in the bag that the nurse brought to me. We might be able to get some idea of what the patient was given…but…" He caught up to her, trying to make sense of what she was saying. "Abby, are you saying you saw another doctor inject Hancock with medication? *Here?* Not in the patient's room?"

Click.

The doors behind them, the ones they'd come through,

closed tight. The lock popped and the sound of it echoed down the dead, dark corridor. It was pitch-black.

Abby shuddered against Blake's supportive arm.

"Let's get you back. I think you've remembered enough for now." Blake started to redirect them the way that they'd come. "I'm sure someone will hear us if we knock."

But Abby pulled against him. "We are much closer to the stairwell. You said that's where the custodian found me, right?"

"Right." Blake shook his head, following behind her in the darkness. "Really, please, let me get you back to that wheelchair.... Are all Amish women this stubborn?"

"Most are much worse." She pushed open the door of the stairwell. There was some dim lighting.

"I'll keep that in mind in case I have any more Amish patients." Blake linked an arm gently under hers, supporting most of her weight. He led her carefully down the stairs. Shadows seemed to dance above them in the dim lighting. Twice she stopped and looked up.

"Do you...?" Were his eyes playing tricks on him? He could have sworn he saw someone above them. A shadow. A movement. Someone dressed in white.

"Yes," Abby said. "I see little..."

Blake frowned at her words. She was seeing it, too. He wasn't imagining them. A shadow passed over the wall beside them. "Lights? Shadows?"

She nodded. They continued a few more steps.

He tried to hurry her down to the ground floor. "I'm sure it's nothing. I guess our eyes are not adjusting to the bad lighting."

A loud clanging sounded overhead. Abby, startled by the sound, slipped on the next step. Blake helped straighten and steady her. He had to get her back to bed. She was about to collapse.

Clang. Metal against metal. Louder and louder. Something was falling. The sound echoed through the space, coming closer and closer.

He looked up, as did Abby, who was growing faint. He could feel her legs buckling. Blake wrapped himself around her and pushed them both under the cover of the second-floor landing. Something was coming down in a hurry and they had to move or get hit.

A magnificent crash sounded behind him.

A stainless-steel surgical tray landed in the very spot where they'd stood, complete with an assortment of sharp scalpels and other surgical instruments, which rattled down around them like a metal rainstorm.

Once the stairs were quiet, Blake lifted his hands to Abby's shoulders. "You okay?"

"No. I'm not." Her body trembled under his hands as she shook her head from side to side. "I think someone is trying to kill me."

THREE

An hour later, Blake's thoughts were swimming as he sat with Abby and two policemen in a special conference room of the hospital. The more time they spent going over the particulars of the assault and the incident in the stairwell, the more confused he felt.

He shook his head. Nothing seemed to make sense these days. His parents' accident. The revelation of his adoption. His inheritance. His arrival in Lancaster to search for his birth parents. He couldn't even decide if he wanted to find his birth parents or not…and he might not have a choice. The search, after all, could very well lead to nothing.

Then again, it could change his life.

Blake wasn't sure which of those results he wanted. The future seemed so muddled. He wasn't used to that.

In any case, working on his search wouldn't be happening today. He wasn't even sure if he would be able to leave the hospital anytime soon. The more he and Abby repeated their stories to the police, the crazier and crazier the whole thing sounded. If it hadn't actually happened to him, he would not have believed it himself.

"And the name of the patient that died from cardiac arrest?" Chief McClendon scratched his thinning red hair.

He was tall and lean and looked like a man you did not want to cross.

"Hancock. Nicolas Hancock." Blake shook his head. "I had an extra copy of his transfer chart, but I left it on the wheelchair when we went to the stairwell, and—"

"Someone swiped it," Abby said. "That was right before the tray of scalpels came down on us."

"Right. By the time I got back up to the third floor to make another copy, the original chart was gone, too. And the bag containing the IV and tubing that I'd left with the wheelchair, as well." Blake felt his phone buzz yet again. A friend, a colleague, a lawyer from New York, no doubt. He silenced the phone.

"So no chart? And now it seems there's no body, either?" the chief repeated. "No evidence that the man was here at all, except for the testimony from you and the crash team, and the bruising and wounds inflicted on Miss Miller after the alleged injection took place."

"I did go to the morgue," Blake continued. "And no... there's no Nicolas Hancock. The autopsist said he'd never gotten the body. And now if you check in the hospital's electronic files, you cannot even find the name Nicolas Hancock in the system."

"But his name was there earlier?"

"Yes, I checked it this afternoon. Before Miss Miller woke up in the E.R. I couldn't figure out how I was assigned to this patient I'd never seen. I thought I might see another doctor's name in there."

"And did you?"

"No."

"Sorry, I'm late to the meeting." A small-framed, middle-aged doctor hurried into the room. He moved with sharp gestures as he made his way around the room and shook hands with everyone. "I'm Dr. Dodd. I'm the head administrator of Fairview Hospital and I'm just flabbergasted at the events that have happened here today. Has anyone called the media?"

"No," said Chief McClendon. "And that better not happen, either."

"Don't worry." Dr. Dodd pressed his dark-framed glasses up the bridge of his nose. "I'll see to it that it doesn't. Hancock's body is in autopsy. I'll make sure the findings are not released to the public. Dr. Jamison, in the interim, your actions today will be under review. I understand both of you will be taking a few days off. I've already made arrangements for that. Now, if you don't have anything else for me, I have another meeting to attend. Please let my custodial staff know when they can reopen the stairwell. Keeping it shut off is a safety violation, you know."

"You have the body?" Blake asked.

"Of course. It's in autopsy. But naturally, you won't see the report until it gets to me and the authorities."

"I guess I don't understand why I'm under review." Blake frowned. He really wished he'd been able to save that IV tubing and possibly prove that someone had caused Hancock's death. "Hancock was dead when I arrived to his room. I'd never seen him before that. The nurses can confirm this. Whatever happened to him—" he looked at Abby "—it happened before I saw him."

"No worries, Dr. Jamison." Dr. Dodd smiled. "It's just a formality. All part of the paperwork."

"You have his chart?"

"Of course we have his chart." Dodd looked annoyed.

"I'll need a copy of that," McClendon said. "Thank you."

"Is that all?"

McClendon nodded. Dr. Dodd scrambled out of the room as quickly as he'd come in.

"I guess you didn't look in the right places, Dr. Jamison," said McClendon. "Then again, you *are* new here."

Blake shook his head. He was new—he wasn't stupid. He knew how to look up files and find a body in a morgue. He'd even spoken to the autopsist. He didn't like the idea of this review. And he definitely didn't like Dr. Dodd. Something was fishy about this whole mess, and in situations like this, the administration usually looked for a scapegoat to blame. Blake had a sinking feeling Dodd meant for that scapegoat to be him.

McClendon tapped more notes into his tablet, then looked to his younger colleague. "Langer, head to the morgue. See what you can find out. Get that file. Then question the crash team and every nurse who came in contact with Nicolas Hancock. Even talk to the person who added his data to the hospital patient files. Somebody has to know something. Do not mention the word *murder* or either the doctor's or Abigail's names. I don't want any of this leaking out."

"Yes, sir." Langer, who was built like a pit bull and was probably just as feisty, spun away from the hospital conference room and headed to the elevators.

McClendon stowed his tablet inside his front jacket pocket. "This is a delicate situation. While we want to cover all of our bases, the person we are looking for could very well work in the hospital. This isn't the kind of person we want to cause to panic. That could make the situation more dangerous.

"Now, we know that Miss Miller was assaulted and drugged. If your Hancock and her Hancock are one and the same, then it sounds like you both could be in a lot of danger."

"We witnessed a murder, right?"

Abby's blunt assessment of the day's events hit Blake

like a ton of bricks. Murder? *Unbelievable*—Abby had witnessed a murder. And to some extent so had he. Blake could hardly wrap his head around it all.

"Right," McClendon agreed. "From what Dr. Dodd said, it sounds like the two of you will have the next few days off. My advice is for you both to keep your distance from the hospital until we see what kind of information we can pull together."

He moved toward Blake and placed a card in his hand. "I'll be in touch. Make sure Miss Miller gets safely home." The chief tipped his head to Abigail, then left them alone in the conference room.

Blake stared after the chief for a long moment. What a day. He could barely take it all in. He was exhausted. And he could only imagine that Abby must be even more so, considering all the abuse her body had taken. Of course, if she'd just stayed in her bed in the E.R., some of the trouble could have been avoided.

He turned back to Miss Abigail Miller. Looked as if he was to give her a ride home. Frankly, he was glad to have the excuse to keep an eye on her a bit longer. She'd pushed herself too hard today and needed someone to make sure she went straight home and got some rest. Although as tough and stubborn as she was, she probably already had her own ideas about that.

He wouldn't admit to himself that he found the woman's ridiculous determination rather intriguing. Or that he found her pretty, too. Naturally pretty, not like many of the women he knew back in New York who spent a lot of money in order to look a certain way. Abby had smooth, creamy skin, huge blue eyes and a healthy glow, despite the lump on her head. And her energy—it was amazing. It drew everyone in—or at least, it drew him in.

Blake made a note to himself to be on his guard with

Abby. Not only was she a patient, he had not come to Lancaster for romance. In fact, that was the *last* thing he needed in his life.

"I'm disappointed," she said. "I'd hoped there would be more they could do. And it all sounded so crazy as I was retelling what happened, you know?"

"Crazy but real. As real as whoever put those nasty bruises on you. Now that the body is in the morgue, I'm sure the investigation will move right along." Blake rubbed his hand through his hair. He didn't want to think about it anymore. He wanted dinner and a long, hot shower. "Let's get out of here."

"Am I allowed out of here?" She stood, too, a hopeful and wide-eyed expression on her face.

Blake smiled. "I already signed the release. But as I'm sure you already know, after a concussion you shouldn't spend the night alone. Someone has to be with you and wake you up at certain intervals during the night."

"Right." She let out a long sigh. "I guess I'll go to Eli's."

Was Eli a boyfriend? Abby definitely wasn't married. Everyone had been calling her *Miss* Miller. Blake shook his head. Why was he even thinking about that? "You shouldn't drive, either. You've had a lot of medication today."

She checked her watch and frowned. "Hmm...that's a problem. Janice has already gone home and most of my other friends and family drive buggies."

"I'm staying at the Willow Trace Bed-and-Breakfast. Are you headed in that direction?"

"Actually, that's not far from where my brother lives," she said. "Would you mind terribly?"

"Eli is your brother?" He lifted an eyebrow.

"Yes, and he drives a buggy, or I'd ask him to pick me up himself." She smiled. She had a fabulous smile. "He used to drive a Mustang, but now he's back to a buggy…. So, do I get a ride or what?"

"Oh, yes. Of course." Blake felt his face flood with heat. "I thought I already said that."

Abby collected her things from her nurse's locker and followed the new doctor to his car—one very expensive SUV.

Hochmut—that was what her father would say if he saw her in that fancy vehicle. Bishop Miller would shake his head and disapprove, just as he seemed to do of everything she decided these days. Her father didn't know how much his condemnation hurt—she wouldn't let it show. She couldn't.

Anyway, it would be silly not to take the ride from the doctor. He was headed in the same direction. And hopefully, her father would not be visiting when she arrived at her brother's.

Blake drove slowly out of the hospital parking lot. Almost immediately, they came up behind an Amish buggy. Abby sighed. Looked as if it might be a long, slow drive to Eli's.

"This highway is not a good one for passing," Abby said.

Blake was just about to reply when his phone rang. Again. It was almost nonstop—buzzing, ringing, vibrating. What could be so important?

"Sounds like someone needs to get in touch with you very badly," she said.

"Excuse me," he said to her, then answered the phone. "Hello…No, I can't…I'm not in the city.…I don't know.… You'll just have to figure it out.…Not anytime soon.… Okay…Bye."

He put the device away.

"I'm sorry. People back home keep forgetting I'm not in town. It's crazy. It's ringing all the time." He looked embarrassed or flustered or both. "In a few days it will slow down...I hope."

"So, getting away from all of that—is that one of your *reasons* for coming to Lancaster?" she asked. "Or are you interested in the countryside? The Amish? Horses and buggies? Avoiding a nightmare family you left behind?"

He laughed at her teasing. He was quite handsome when he smiled. Abby turned away as a strange rush of emotions shot through her.

"All of those things." He looked at his phone. "I guess some things are harder to get away from than others. But I don't have any family."

"Everyone has family."

"I don't."

She glanced over at him, waiting for an explanation.

"Only child. And my parents died recently."

Abby dropped her head. "I'm so sorry. I didn't mean to bring up something so—"

"No, no. It's fine. The accident was months ago," he said.

"I'm still very sorry." Abby turned and looked out the window. "Can I ask what kind of accident?"

"A plane crash." Blake relaxed his hands on the beautiful mahogany steering wheel. "You know, one of those little island-hopper planes. The computer inside malfunctioned. They hit a storm. It just happened. It wasn't anyone's fault."

"You must miss them terribly."

He smiled, but it was a sad, regretful sort of smile that touched Abby's heart at its core.

"So what else? You said you came to Lancaster for lots

of reasons. So tell me a few. To get away from your phone and what else?"

"Well, the rest of it is a long story." He smiled at her again. "But *you,* you are doing remarkably well after all you've been through today."

"Thanks, but I feel like a wreck. A train wreck, actually. I can't wait to get to my brother's and collapse."

There was a moment of silence.

"So, another reason you came to Fairview?" she prodded him, not liking the silence. "Come on. It takes my mind off the assault."

"Okay, another reason... Actually, I was going to tell you earlier but then we started talking about... Never mind." He shook his head. "So another reason I came to Lancaster is to find something. I might have a family connection here I plan to look up."

"But I thought you didn't have any family."

"Well, I don't. I don't know these people. And it may be nothing. Really, forget I mentioned it." He changed the subject. "Did you need to stop by your own place? You must need to get some things? Some clothes? A toothbrush?"

"Oh, no. That's okay. I can borrow things from my sister-in-law." She hadn't thought about going by her place, but he was right. She really did need to at some point. Still, she didn't want to impose, nor did she want to take any longer than necessary to get to Eli's. She was still quite unsettled after the day's events.

"I really don't mind," he said.

He seemed sincere, so Abby decided to infringe on his kindness a bit further. The more she thought about it, if she didn't go by her house, then Eli would have to, and that would upset Hannah and get the night off to a bad start. "Actually, if you really wouldn't mind, it would give me a chance to check on Zoe, Chloe and Blue-jeans."

"Zoe, Chloe and Blue-jeans?" He shot her a furtive look.

"My two cats and my horse."

"You have a horse?"

"Yes, and a buggy, too. I couldn't decide if I wanted to sell it or not." Abby glanced at Blake. His big, chocolate eyes were soft and smiling. The rest of him was stiff and businesslike. At the hospital he'd been like that, too—two-sided. One very kind. The other standoffish. She wondered which message was the true Blake.

"I would love to ride in a horse and buggy," he said.

"Well, when I'm feeling better, I'd be happy to take you out in mine." Abby stopped as the words sank in. To an Amish man, an invitation like that would sound as if she was inviting him on a courting date. Fortunately, the doctor wasn't Amish and would take the invitation in the spirit it was given—as a friendly gesture and nothing more.

"Sounds like a plan," he said. "Thank you. And of course, you should check on your animals. You should have said so. You live on a farm? You must have some land if you have a horse, right? This is all new to me. I've lived my whole life in an apartment on the Upper East Side."

The upper east side of what? Am I supposed to know what he's talking about? "It's not a farm," she said. "I mean it is. But I don't farm anything. I run a clinic. I lease the land out to a real farmer.... Sorry. I'm rambling."

Following her directions, Blake maneuvered his way slowly around the buggy that they'd been stuck behind for the past quarter mile. A few minutes later, they pulled up in front of her home and clinic.

"I'll be quick." She hopped out of the car but paused when she saw how dark the house was. If it hadn't been for the headlights of Blake's car, they wouldn't have been able to see a thing.

"Is something wrong?" He parked in her semicircle

driveway, leaving his headlights to shine over the front porch.

"I don't think so." She forced a smile and searched in her bag for the house key. A feeling of dread passed through her. She couldn't shake the feeling that something was wrong here, but she tried to ignore it. Likely it was nothing more than nerves—hardly surprising after the day she'd had. "I guess the sensors on my porch lights are broken? Those lights usually come on when it gets dark."

"Let me come up to the door with you, just to be safe. You weren't too steady on your feet earlier and shouldn't be stumbling around in the dark." He turned off the engine, but left his headlights on to shine over the front porch. "What a great house."

"Thanks." Abby fumbled with her key, taking what seemed like an interminably long time to unlock the door. Blake stood back as she went in and reached for the lights. Nothing happened as she flicked the light switch.

"Looks like the power is out." She headed across the dark space to a small hutch. She tried to turn on a small lamp. Nothing. "Yep, it must be the power. I have a flashlight in the bottom drawer here. Once we get to the kitchen, I can check the electrical panel. Just a second."

Abby rummaged through the drawers of the hutch. "I know that flashlight is—"

Blake's hand came down on her shoulder, giving her a chill.

"Shh," he whispered. "There's someone else in the house."

Abby swallowed hard as her hands finally landed around the flashlight she'd been looking for. Turning it on, she pointed it down the hallway in time to see a dark shadow flash across the entrance to her kitchen. Blake's hand swiftly eased the light from her hand.

"Stay here," he said before taking off toward the dark figure.

Abby wasn't about to stand there in the dark. She followed right behind him, feeling a cold blast of night air blow over her as she entered the kitchen. Blake flashed the light in every direction. The back door was wide open. Whoever the intruder had been, he'd escaped without a sound.

FOUR

Abby rushed for the open door, but Blake grabbed her arm and pulled her back. After the day they'd had, he wasn't too sure running out into the darkness after the unknown was a good idea. Better to fix whatever had been done to the electricity. It would be much easier to spot the intruder with the floodlights on.

"I thought I told you to stay put."

"I didn't want to stay back there in the dark by myself."

Blake couldn't argue with her reasoning, even though he was pretty certain he'd never met anyone as hardheaded as Abby Miller. In any case, he'd spotted her circuit-breaker panel a few feet from the door. The door to the panel had been opened as if someone had been making adjustments.

"Maybe the power wasn't off after all. Looks like someone's been messing with your breakers. Here, take this." He handed the flashlight to her. "Shine the light this way."

Blake opened the metal panel. As he'd suspected, the main breaker had been turned off. He flipped it back to the "on" position. Abby was right beside him, turning on both the inside and outside lights. The backyard lit up. Together they scanned the area from the back stoop. Blake saw open fields, a run-in shed and a horse grazing in a large paddock. No intruder.

"I guess we surprised whoever it was and he left."

"I hope so," Blake said. "But let's check the rest of the house anyway."

Room by room, Blake followed Abby through the house. Nothing looked out of order. When they reached the foyer again, Blake noticed an interior door that in the darkness he hadn't seen behind the front entrance. The sign on the door read Abigail Miller, R.N. and Certified Midwife, Consultation, Mondays and Wednesdays 12–4. "Impressive."

"Thanks. I went all-out when I designed the clinic. I wanted to bring the best to Willow Trace." She walked past him. "And this door was locked when I left for the hospital this morning. I'm certain of that."

Blake followed her into the clinic and saw that Abigail had built a state-of-the-art facility inside the old cottage. It had been thoughtfully and tastefully done and unlike the rest of the house, which had been so simple and plain, everything here spoke of modern medicine and technology. In its usual state, it was unquestionably very impressive. Right now, it looked like a disaster area. Abby gasped as she staggered forward. Broken glass crunched under her feet. The examining area had been trashed. Boxes of supplies had been strewn across the space. All the shelves had been stripped and their contents spilled all over the table, counters and flooring.

Tears streamed down her face. He could tell she was trying to wipe them away before he could see, but they wouldn't stop. "I'm sorry. I'm just so tired. And this is so unbelievable.... Two weeks ago, I decide that my calling is nursing, that I don't want to give it up. I told my family. My father. He's so upset with me. I had such a peace about it...but now? My wonderful clinic that I created just a few years ago has been ruined and I…don't know. I don't know what to do."

Blake knew she wasn't really talking to him, just venting aloud her frustration and fatigue. His heart felt heavy for her. He felt as if the very center of his life had been destroyed, too, when his parents died in that plane crash. He and Abby definitely had something in common—they were both struggling with their direction and their families.

He looked at her standing there sobbing. He had to do something. He couldn't just go on as if she were fine. She was a patient, after all. If a patient were crying, he would give them a hug, right?

Slowly, Blake put his arm around her shoulders and gave her a comforting squeeze. To his great astonishment, Abby turned into his chest and wept against his shoulder. Blake didn't know what to do. Keep hugging her? Push her back? He didn't move. But he couldn't help but catch the soft floral fragrance of her hair and her skin. After a moment, he unfroze himself, slid his hands to her shoulders and pushed her back.

Abigail's embarrassment was evident in her flushed cheeks and splotchy neck. "I'm sorry. I didn't mean to fall apart on you. I'm not usually this…this…"

"You have every right to fall apart." He grazed her cheek with the back of his hand. "I just thought we should call the police. Again."

He pulled out his cell phone and the card that Chief McClendon had passed to him only a few hours earlier. He dialed the number while trying to give Abby a reassuring smile. "Maybe later I can help you clean it up. It's not so bad. Right?"

Abby broke into a watery smile and chuckled. "Right. Not so bad."

As the phone line began to ring, Blake swallowed hard. Abby was like no one he'd ever met—such an odd mixture of independence and vulnerability, of determination and quick wits. He was going to have to be on his guard about more than this person who was after them, because if there was one thing in his life he did not need or have time for, it was romance.

"Abby, I can't believe you didn't send Chief McClendon here to tell me what happened to you today." Her big brother, Eli, paced his kitchen, pulling on his suspenders and shaking his head of thick blond hair as he walked.

"I was coming straight here." She could hardly speak from exhaustion. She couldn't stop shaking and her head throbbed terribly. "Blake was nice enough to swing by my house so that I could pick up some clothes and feed the animals, and that's when we walked in on whoever that was. Anyway, there was no point in telling you sooner. What could you do? There's nothing to do except try to get away from it all and wait for the police to catch the man responsible. And that's why I'm here."

Even though she still felt like a sitting duck. She'd thought being at her brother's would make her feel safe, but instead, she now worried that she and Blake had just brought danger with them.

"I don't know. There's got to be something we can do," Eli said. "Chief McClendon told you to lie low?"

"Not in those exact words." Blake spoke from the corner of the kitchen. Abby blushed at the sound of his voice. She'd hardly been able to look at him after she'd fallen apart at the clinic. Practically jumping into his arms. She wished he'd dropped her off and gone straight back to the bed-and-breakfast. But once Hannah heard they'd had nothing to eat, she wouldn't allow Blake to escape.

"Is McClendon still at your house?" Eli asked.

"I imagine so." Blake's brown eyes were soft again. Not hard and shocked like after the scene at the clinic. "There was an entire crew there, taking pictures and samples."

"That's good. Maybe they'll lift some prints." Eli continued to pace. He was making her dizzy.

"Relax, Eli." Abby gave him a hard stare. "You're not a detective anymore, remember?"

He ignored her. "Was anything missing from your house?"

"Nothing in the house—not that I noticed, anyway. But in the clinic. Most of my medicines were sabotaged. Opened. Slashed. Contaminated. And oddly they stole all my epi-packs."

"Epi-packs?"

Blake cleared his throat. "They're for people with severe allergies. Like an emergency kit. The EpiPen is a small dose of epinephrine, which prevents an allergy from sending someone into anaphylactic shock. They have saved a lot of parents trips to the hospitals and even saved lives. Epinephrine is the same drug that I believe was given to Abigail and to Mr. Hancock to send them into cardiac arrest."

"So too much of a good drug can kill?" Eli asked.

"Exactly," Blake said. "And epinephrine is not traceable like other drugs in the body because it is produced naturally."

"What's strange to me is that this person took the epi-packs *after* he killed Hancock. What was the point of that?" Abby said. "And the amount of epinephrine he dosed me with was way more than what is in an epi-pack. Clearly, he has access to the drug on his own, so why steal my packs?"

"He's probably trying to scare you. Or throw off the investigation." Eli stroked his short beard. "It takes everyone's eyes off the hospital for a while. Maybe there is unfinished business there."

"Like killing patients in dark hallways?" Abby said.

"We must get ahead of this guy instead of behind him. The first attempt when he drugged you was serious. He was feeling powerful. But the stairwell and the break-in seem more like scare tactics. He's not as confident as he was and we should try to keep it that way."

"How do we get ahead of this person? We don't know who he is or where he is," Abby said.

Eli looked up at her with a hopeful expression. "You can describe him, right?"

"Not really." Abby shook her head. "He was wearing scrubs and a mask. I saw his eyes. That's about it."

"Well, the perpetrator could be anyone, not necessarily a doctor from the hospital. But if you have an idea of his size, his voice, skin color—with the computers the composite artists use now, you wouldn't believe how well they can narrow down a suspect list."

"Not tonight." Abby held up her hand. She couldn't take any more talk about the situation. Her brother meant well but he did not seem to understand what an ordeal she had been through.

Blake stepped forward. "I would have to agree. She needs rest."

Her brother turned to Blake, then back to her. Abby hid a grin—another man having an opinion about her welfare had definitely thrown her brother off-kilter.

"Essa!" Hannah placed several plates in the center of the table and waved them all over. "Time to eat. Everyone to the table."

Eli led them in a prayer of thanksgiving. Abby could have listened to his words all night. Eli was a true man of God—he knew where his strength came from. And what kind of man was Blake? At the amen, she glanced at him. Were those tears in his eyes? She watched him wipe them away quickly as he dug into his dinner. This was one man she did not understand—he seemed to change more than the weather and she'd only known him for one day.

"Wow. This is wonderful." Blake had a faraway look in his eyes as he complimented her family on the house and the dinner.

"So, Blake…" Hannah started. "You're a doctor at Fairview?"

"Yes. Well, temporarily."

"And you're from New York?"

"Yes."

Eli slapped the table. "Didn't you say the patient Hancock was from New York, too?"

Abby nodded with a smile. Her brother could barely contain himself. He was concerned for her, but he was also reliving his work as a Philadelphia police detective. It was not too long ago he'd come home on a case to help Hannah find the men that had killed her stepdaughter. In the end, he'd decided to stay and leave his *Englischer* life behind, but his years of training and experience as a detective were still a part of him. He let out a long sigh. "I really need to talk to McClendon."

"Well, that's not happening tonight," Hannah said. "No calls in the house. Let's just have a nice, relaxing dinner and worry about all of that tomorrow."

Blake's phone sounded almost simultaneously with Hannah's reminder of the no-cell-phones rule. Blake grabbed his phone from his pocket and silenced it. "Sorry. I'll just turn it off. I didn't even realize how much I'm on my phone until I came here. I guess back in New York, everyone is, so no one thinks anything about it. I think tomorrow I may just leave it in my hotel room."

"Well, not a bad idea, Dr. Jamison. We don't use them in this house." Hannah's tone was kind but firm.

"Don't feel bad," Eli said, teasing his wife. "She asked me to get rid of my gun. A cell phone is nothing."

Hannah waved away her husband's words. "Speaking of your life back in New York, Dr. Jamison...you're not married, are you?"

"No. I'm not." Hannah's tone had sounded a slight bit chastising. "Is that a problem?"

"Of course not," Abby said, glaring at Hannah so that she would not continue with the same topic. "It's just a common topic around here. With the Amish. Especially among the women."

Hannah looked indignant. "Oh, don't mind me. I'm just getting to know our guest. What brings you here to Willow Trace, Dr. Jamison?"

Blake had just shoved a large forkful of meat into his mouth and couldn't answer.

"Blake has family here, don't you, Blake?" Abby smiled. She'd purposely caught him off guard. Now he would have to answer what she'd been trying to figure out all day—why was Dr. Jamison at Fairview Hospital?

Blake swallowed down the lump of stew before he could answer. He'd almost rather talk about his pathetic love life than about why he was in Lancaster. "Maybe. I said that maybe I have a family connection in Lancaster."

There was clearly another question bubbling inside of Abigail, but a knock at the door sounded before she could get it out.

Eli excused himself from the table to get the door. Hannah hopped up to take care of the dishes. Blake and Abby tried to follow but Hannah stopped them.

"Go on into the other room." Hannah shooed them away

like little flies. "Both of you. Sounds like we have visitors. I'll see to the kitchen. Go on. Go relax and visit. You've both done enough today."

Blake followed Abby into the living area, which, like the rest of the home, was tastefully but simply decorated. The walls were undecorated, simply painted a shade of light blue. All of the big windows were covered with green shades and simple white curtains. There were a few dim lamps set on handmade wooden tables. A sofa and several lightly upholstered chairs were placed about in an orderly circle.

Eli stoked the fire while his newly arrived guests sat together on the couch—a young couple holding a sleeping baby while their older child stood against his father. The boy stared wide-eyed at Blake and Abby as they entered the room.

"Mary!" Abigail rushed forward. She hugged the young mother and swept the sleeping child from her arms. "Little Levi. Oh, isn't he just beautiful? And, Stephen, you are so grown up—*sehr grose.*"

The little boy straightened up from his position against his father, standing tall and proud.

"Jonathan and Mary, this is Blake Jamsion—a doctor at the hospital. Blake, this is the Zook family. Mary and I have been friends all our lives. Her parents own the bed-and-breakfast where you are staying."

Blake shook hands with the couple, admiring their Amish dress, which matched Eli's and Hannah's exactly— trousers, suspenders and simply cut shirts for the men, plain blue dresses and black aprons for the women. Little Stephen wore a miniature version of the grown men's clothing. He whispered something to his father, then took off out the front door.

"He likes to visit all of Eli's stock. We don't have the

cattle Eli has here. He's fascinated by it," Jonathan explained. He had the same peculiar, square beard as Eli did, only around the jawline. No mustache. A strange and unique look. Blake couldn't remember seeing anything like it before.

Mary's hair, like Hannah's, was tucked up in a white *Kapp*. He glanced at Abigail and her long blond braid, maybe a little glad it wasn't hidden under a *Kapp*. He wondered what it might look like loose and free-flowing.

"We heard you had some trouble up at the hospital," Jonathan said.

"*Ja,* you could say that." Abby spun around with the tiny infant. "How did you hear?"

The couple explained how the news had spread from the hospital to another couple from the church to their neighbors. "We didn't know if Eli had heard, so we thought we should come over. We knew he'd want to know about his sister. We should have figured you'd be here telling him yourself."

"I'm glad you came. It's good to see you and the children. Just what I needed to get my mind off this afternoon."

Some conversation passed in Pennsylvania Dutch. Blake sat back and listened to the lilting, rolling language. He didn't know if the talk was about him or the happenings at the hospital, but either way the language relaxed him. Called to him. Could it be that Amish blood ran through his veins? If he hadn't been put up for adoption, could he have grown up in a room like this instead of in a penthouse that overlooked Central Park?

"Well, at least you didn't go to the bishop." Abby broke back into English.

"Oh, but we did." Mary smiled. "We passed by there on the way here. He hadn't heard. He is very concerned. He would have been over to see you himself if he had not already had some other church business to attend to tonight. He assumed your brother would be looking after you as soon as he heard the news. But you should expect the bishop in the morning."

"Danki."

Even Blake could tell Abby was not happy about this news. She was not pleased that this bishop person knew her business.

"So, who is the bishop? Is he an elder of the church?" Blake asked.

Eli and Jonathan smiled at him. They looked at Abby. Everyone seemed to be holding back a laugh.

Except for Abigail. She turned, a sad frown under her big blue eyes. "The bishop is the leader of the *Ordnung*. The leader of the Amish church. He's also my father."

There was a second of silence over the room then the front door burst open like a bomb had blown it off its hinges. Little Stephen came running inside. He was pale and out of breath, and his hat was missing.

"What is it, Stephen?" his mother asked.

Her son ran into her arms, letting loose an onslaught of tears he'd bravely held back until that moment. He told his parents what had happened. Again, Blake couldn't understand the Amish language. But he watched as the rest of the people in the room reacted grimly to the boy's tale.

Whatever he said, it was not happy news. Several times they all looked at Abigail, who'd grown pale. As the boy finished, Abby put a hand to her head as if it ached worse than ever.

Eli stood and put a hand on his sister's shoulder. He nodded to Jonathan, and the two men headed for the door.

"Is something wrong? Can I help?" Blake stood with the other men.

Eli turned back, his expression bleak. "Someone is in

the stable. He grabbed little Stephen and told him to go back to the house. He told him to tell Miss Miller that he is watching."

FIVE

Blake awoke early in his cozy bed at the bed-and-breakfast, his thoughts on Abby Miller and the string of strange events that occurred the day before. Someone had poisoned her and left her for dead on that empty third-floor wing of the hospital. That someone had already successfully killed Mr. Hancock, the transfer patient from New York, while manipulating the hospital's computer systems. Probably that same someone had dumped a tray of scalpels over their heads, broken into Abigail's clinic and sent a threatening message to her via a small Amish child, who'd been scared out of his wits.

Blake could not forget the horror on Abby's face as that child had told the others what had happened in the stable. She had looked beaten down. As her brother had pointed out later, that was most likely the man's intention—to beat her down until he caught up with her and eliminated her for catching him at the scene of the crime.

Eli and Jonathan had raced back to the barn after Stephen had returned, but whoever had spoken to the child had been long gone. Most strange was that the man had spoken Pennsylvania Dutch to the boy, realizing he was too young to understand English. This meant that whoever was after Abigail was close enough to the Plain folk to know their language. That narrowed down the list of suspects in Blake's mind. But Eli and McClendon had pointed out that it was very possible that more than one person was involved in all of this. Without a motive for the murder of Hancock, it was going to be very difficult to come up with an actual list of suspects. And how could they find a motive when there was no information about Hancock? He was a New Yorker with no known family or connections. Blake was afraid it would be a long time before the police got to the bottom of this affair, and that meant a long time before he and Abby could go back to the hospital.

Anyway, it was all so disturbing. Blake felt he was tied to these events in a way that went deeper than simply his name on Hancock's chart. But why, he couldn't say. It was probably nothing but silly conjecture on his part.

It was still early, but knowing he wouldn't sleep anymore with so much on his mind, Blake had a quick shower and shave. The he dressed in jeans and an oxford before sitting down at the small corner desk where he'd plugged in his laptop. A hundred-plus emails loaded into his inbox. He had let them accumulate over the past three days while he'd been busy with his new job—now he had to deal with messages from his partners in his medical practice, from his friends in New York and from Natalie. The same people who kept texting and calling and needing him for this or that.

He had left New York without a lot of fanfare. None of his Manhattan friends knew the real reason he'd come to Willow Trace—not even Natalie, who had, at one time, been his fiancée. Things between them had ended before he lost his parents and found out the truth about his background, so not even she knew why he felt he needed to be here. And that was the way he wanted to keep it. For now. This was something he wanted to explore on his own.

Strange how it didn't bother him that he'd almost told Abby after only knowing her for a few hours. Just like he didn't care that she'd seen him shed a tear during the prayer. In New York, there had never been time or space to think over his real emotions, but here they seemed to surface without warning. Like his attraction to Abby. Something he'd have to keep a lid on. He was only in Lancaster to get away and explore his past. It was definitely temporary. He was not here to complicate his life with a romance. He had enough of those sorts of complications back home.

Blake closed his laptop and pushed it aside. With a trembling hand, he unfolded the beautifully penned sheet of linen stationery he kept in a folder in his laptop case. Mr. Pooler, his mother's lawyer, had given him the letter on his thirtieth birthday. Only two months after the accident.

Dearest son,
Happy birthday! If you are reading this letter, that means your father and I have left this world. Please know you have been our greatest gift during this life and nothing but a source of joy for us. But, as I think you suspected, I did not give birth to you. I could not have children and so your father and I adopted you. We never told you this simply because you never asked and we were perfectly content to keep you all to ourselves. However, we always agreed that we would tell you all we know when you turned thirty. It is not much. We only know that your parents were Amish and lived in Willow Trace, Pennsylvania. They were married and could not keep you for financial reasons.

The adoption was handled through a lawyer by the name of Anthony Linton, Esquire, of Lancaster County. He can reveal the names if you so desire. If

you want to get in touch with your birth parents, then
we understand and fully support your decision. Just
know that no matter what, we love you, and we're so
very proud of you. Happy birthday, dearest.
Your mother, Sarah

After six months, the letter still brought tears to Blake's
eyes. He refolded it and placed it back into the file folder.
This was the reason he'd come. But was he ready to begin
the search for his biological parents? He wasn't sure. Without the encouragement from his own mother, he might not
have even ventured into Lancaster. But after his visit last
night to the Millers' home, Blake decided to make that
first step. He had a few hours before he was due to pick
up Abby and head over to her place to clean up the mess
from the break-in. He didn't have an appointment with the
lawyer his mother had mentioned. He hadn't had time to
call, given his schedule at the hospital. But he didn't see
the harm in driving over to Linton's office and popping in.

An hour later, Blake drove through another section of
Lancaster, following the directions of his GPS to Linton's
law office. The area was extremely commercialized in
contrast to the quiet country appeal of Willow Trace. He'd
driven right into the thick of morning traffic. It was nothing compared to Manhattan and still he frowned. His easy,
relaxing drive from the bed-and-breakfast to the hospital
had already spoiled him.

It was a little after ten when he located the strand of
connected offices. Linton's was sandwiched between a
dentist and dermatologist. Blake parked his Land Rover
at the end of the building and took a deep breath. Was it
possible he'd know the names of his birth parents today?
Did he even want to know them and meet them?

Blake's heart pounded against his rib cage. He took up

a folder containing not only his mother's letter but also some other documentation of identification and a thorough inquiry, which his mother's lawyer had conducted, verifying Mr. Linton and the adoption. There was even a head shot of the lawyer himself. Blake steadied himself and entered the drab office.

"May I help you?" asked a woman seated at the front desk. She looked mid-fifties and had a motherly way to her. The rest of the reception area consisted of empty space and two empty armchairs. Behind her was another office. The light was on and Blake could hear a man's voice from within. But the door was pulled nearly closed, blocking anyone outside from looking in or hearing any of the conversation.

Blake approached the receptionist with his folder tucked under his arm. "Hello, I was hoping to speak with Mr. Linton."

"We don't take solicitors here." Her voice was kind but also firm.

"Oh, no. I'm not selling anything. I want to consult Mr. Linton about a legal matter."

The woman's fixed smile didn't change. "Mr. Linton is not currently taking new clients. I'd be happy to furnish you with a list of alternative lawyers in the area."

Blake swallowed hard. Why was it so hard for him to just say why he was there? "I'm sorry. Let's start over.... I'm Dr. Blake Jamison. I'm from New York and I already have a lawyer. I'm here because I recently found out that I was adopted and that Mr. Linton handled the adoption. I have a letter and some documentation from my lawyer asking Mr. Linton to please release the names of my birth parents to me."

The woman was no longer smiling, but she wasn't dismissing him, either. She stood and motioned to one of the armchairs to her left. "Have a seat, Dr. Jamison. I'll be right back."

She disappeared through the door to the back office and closed it. This was it. Blake was going to learn the names of his real parents. He wiped his sweaty palms over the tops of his slacks and sat impatiently awaiting her return.

After a few minutes, the woman came back into the reception area, carefully closing the door to the office behind her. Her face was pale, but she once again pressed a practiced smile over her lips.

"It's just as I expected." She shook her head regretfully. "This has happened before. You have the wrong Mr. Linton. This Mr. Linton does not, nor has he ever, handled adoptions. I'm so sorry."

Blake's heart fell into his stomach. How could that be true? It wasn't. He'd researched Mr. Linton. His parents' lawyer had verified the information in the letter, as well. What was this woman hiding, and why?

Blake stood and faced the woman. There was deceit in her pale blue eyes. "I don't think I'm mistaken. I have documents here stating that Mr. Anthony Linton of this address is indeed the lawyer who handled my adoption thirty years ago."

He started to open the folder, but the woman waved away his documents.

"Perhaps if I could speak directly to Mr. Linton?" Blake asked.

"I'm afraid that's not possible." She turned back to her desk and took her seat. "Mr. Linton is not available. As I told you, he's not seeing new clients or taking new appointments."

Further discussion would clearly be useless. He would have to go about this a different way. Perhaps by contacting his parents' lawyer again.

"I'm sorry to trouble you." He turned toward the front doors, pulling his cell from his pocket. As he stepped out onto the sidewalk, a black BMW with New York plates peeled through the parking lot at Mach speed. The driver had a long, narrow face. His hair was silvery-white, cut close to the scalp, and he wore a dark suit.

It was Mr. Pooler—his mother's lawyer.

With his cell already in his hands, Blake found Pooler's number in his contacts and hit the call button. Something strange was going on here between the murder, his adoption and the scalpels down the stairs, and he was determined to get answers any way he could.

Abigail brushed and rebrushed her hair in a trancelike state. She had not slept well. Hannah had woken her up periodically as Dr. Jamison had instructed. Each time, the shock of waking had sent her into a panic. The terror was momentary, but the racing pulse and adrenaline rush were hard to recover from. As was the fact that she'd witnessed a murder and nearly been killed herself.

In her mind, everything was unbalanced and felt strange, unfamiliar. Being at her brother's. Not being in an Amish frock. Not having to cover her head or hide her hair under a prayer *Kapp.* She had not realized how those simple things had given her comfort in the past. Her slender jeans and sweater set felt restrictive, clingy and showy. Her mind flashed through scenes from the day before—her attacker grabbing her in the hallway, walking into the trashed clinic and the feel of Blake's strong arms around her. Abby longed to feel comfortable again but she had a feeling that would be a long time coming.

She wished she had not asked Blake to drive her to the hospital to pick up her car. He did not help with the feeling-comfortable issue. For some reason, she couldn't

get a read on him. And she didn't like that. One minute he
was on the phone to New York, driving his fancy car and
being the important new doctor in the E.R. The next minute he was looking at her with those soft brown eyes and
holding her while she fell apart in the clinic. She didn't
usually have so much trouble with figuring people out.

From the bedroom upstairs, she heard gravel churning under the tires of an automobile coming up the drive.
Good. Blake was already there. He was early, which meant
getting everything taken care of even faster. And more important, it meant she could avoid running into her father.
She hurried down the stairs and onto the porch.

But it was not Blake in his large black Land Rover. It
was a police car with Chief McClendon at the wheel and
her brother beside him. Another small car—a silver sports
car—drove directly behind them. Abby's head began to
throb. Had something else happened? She wasn't sure she
wanted to know.

Her brother and the chief got out of the car. From the
small silver sports car emerged a woman, a brunette with
short, spiky hair, looking as if she spent a lot of time at a
gym. From her trunk, she loaded her arms with all sorts
of equipment and headed toward the house.

They all walked up onto the porch together and paused
in front of her.

"This is Carol Ruppert," Chief McClendon told her.
"She's a composite artist from the FBI." Eli offered to
help with her case, but she refused. "She's here to see if
you can remember enough about your attacker to attempt
an identification."

Abby could not stop her frown or her feelings of frustration toward Eli. He should not have gotten involved in
this way. She had already brought danger to Eli's home,
as was proven by the incident at the barn with poor little

Stephen. But this? Bringing the police here? Right into their homes? *This* would really make her father upset. Not to mention the way it would draw attention to them. How had McClendon agreed to this? Especially after practically saying she should hide.

Abby wondered what Blake would have thought of all of this. She wondered if he was safe. She wondered what kind of family connection he had in Lancaster. And why did he seem so sad about it?

Eli was all smiles and optimism as he led everyone inside. Abby was all the more infuriated.

"Eli," she whispered, motioning him to hang back a ways from the other two. He leaned close to her at the kitchen door. She grabbed him by the arm. "Why did you bring them here? You shouldn't get involved in this. What will *Dat* say? Anyway, I didn't really see the man. Remember? Only his eyes."

"You need to quit worrying about *Dat*." Eli shook his arms out of her grasp and placed them on her shoulders. "And worry more about staying alive. Somebody grabbed Stephen in my stable last night. You'd better believe I'm going to do something to find the person responsible."

Abby dropped her head. Eli was right. She had to do whatever she could to help catch this man who'd attacked her, murdered Mr. Hancock and scared poor little Stephen. "But the FBI?"

"They have the most sophisticated system."

Abby still frowned. "We couldn't have done this somewhere else?"

"Hey, I'll take care of *Dat*." Eli turned her toward the kitchen and led her in after the others.

Ms. Ruppert had already begun setting up her high-tech laptop with its very own digital sketchpad at the kitchen table. Abby had never seen anything like it.

She sat across from the woman and answered simple questions, which the artist seemed to have memorized. So many questions. There seemed to be no end to them. Hannah, who had been in her garden, returned and served coffee and pastries to everyone. Chief McClendon took advantage of any pause in the artist's inquiries to ask his own questions.

Abby had plenty of her own, as well.

"Your cats returned to the house soon after you left. One of my officers fed them," the chief said. "And other than the mess in your clinic and the missing epi-packs you reported, the house looked untouched. We didn't lift any prints. Whoever made that mess was wearing gloves. But he did leave footprints outside your back door. We made an impression of those. So far we can only say that he or she was wearing men's shoes and weighed about 170 to 180 pounds. Same sort of footprints in Eli's barn, too."

"Then there must be two men at work. There is no way that doctor at Fairview weighed 180. More like 220. He was a big man."

"What about at the hospital?" Eli asked. "Any news there?"

Before McClendon could respond, Ms. Ruppert beckoned everyone to her monitor. Abby's eyes grew wide. She could not believe how real the computer rendition looked. Everything on the screen was how she remembered it— his eyes and skin tone, even the way his face mask draped over his mouth and nose.

"That's amazing. But how can you match this to anything?"

"Well, the next step is all done by the computer. It will compare different chins and hair, et cetera, to the image. With each new combination, it runs searches through all the databases of online profiles."

"That must take forever."

"It's not a fast process, but it can be useful." Ms. Ruppert packed up her equipment as efficiently as she had assembled it and excused herself. Chief McClendon walked her out.

Abby went to the living room and looked out. She figured her father might be there at any moment and that did not bode well, especially with the chief's car in front of the house. She nearly jumped when she heard another car approaching. It was Blake. He passed Ms. Ruppert in the driveway, then joined McClendon on the steps. Abby could just overhear their words.

"Glad you're here, Jamison," McClendon said in his low baritone. "I've got Hancock's chart and the autopsy report, and frankly, I think you have some serious explaining to do."

Abby scooted away from the window. She hadn't meant to eavesdrop. But what was the chief talking about? Had Blake been hiding information? Was that why she couldn't get a read on him? Had he been untruthful?

Abby dropped her head. The disappointment slammed down on her like a lead weight.

SIX

After the visit to Mr. Linton's office, Blake's mind had been reeling for the past hour. Had he really seen Pooler? Had his mind been playing tricks on him? It was hard to know which way was up.

Blake had left a voice-mail message for Pooler. He'd decided not to accuse him of being in Lancaster, but had spoken only of his difficulty in meeting with Linton. He'd taken a minute to calm down. During that moment he'd remembered that Linton, whom he'd seen a picture of when confirming his office address, and Pooler, his mother's lawyer, were both men in their late fifties with big tufts of gray hair—they would be easy to confuse driving by that quickly. Still pondering what he'd seen, he'd driven straight to the Millers' farm.

He was surprised to find Chief McClendon there. And even more surprised by his accusatory greeting.

"I've told you every single thing I know." Blake stood tall in front of the redheaded Lancaster chief of police. He had nothing to hide. He had done nothing wrong. Perhaps he hadn't shared one of the reasons he'd come to Lancaster, but that had nothing to do with Hancock or Abigail. It was personal—no one's business but his own.

The chief said nothing more on the porch but turned

and went inside. Blake followed. Abigail stood with her back to the doorway of the kitchen. She was dressed in jeans and a sweater. Blake slowed his steps. That nurse's uniform she'd had on the day before had not done her justice. Her big blue eyes glanced back at him as she gave him a nervous half smile. For a second, his anxious thoughts melted away. But after taking a seat next to her at the table, a closer inspection of her face showed the tension around her eyes, reminding him why they were together. It occurred to him that she'd most likely slept worse than he had, and he had slept quite poorly.

She covered her cheeks with a slender hand. "Eli brought a composite artist to the house. She just left. I was surprised what she was able to get from my limited descriptions. How was your morning?"

"Not very productive." Blake swallowed hard. He wanted to share with Abby about his family situation, but this was clearly not the time.

Eli took his seat next to his sister, and Chief McClendon cleared his throat. "We discovered why you weren't able to find the remains of Nicolas Hancock when you visited the morgue. The body was there the entire time, just with no identification. Dr. Dodd admitted later that there are some glitches in the records system at the hospital, which also explains why the electronic chart was unavailable when you tried to look at it. Final report from the autopsist agrees that this patient most likely died from an overdose of epinephrine."

Blake frowned. "But epinephrine wouldn't have been detectable through autopsy."

"No," the chief agreed. "That's not possible. But he ruled out other triggers to the cardiac arrest. The tubing of Mr. Hancock's IV, which you had the nurse save, showed up and was found to contain definite traces of epinephrine. This might not be enough evidence to convince a jury, but with what you both told me yesterday, it convinced me. And since the nursing staff can swear that you, Dr. Jamison, were in surgery at the time that Mr. Hancock was admitted and had never seen the patient before the Code Blue, your review has been closed. Of course, we need both of you to come to the morgue and identify that the body we have is indeed the one you saw yesterday. In the meantime, Lancaster County has officially opened a murder investigation for the death of Nicolas Hancock. Unfortunately, we've had trouble tracking down any information about him."

Abby's spine had gone rigid by midway through the chief's speech. Blake watched her fingers clench into a fist over the unfinished hardwood of the table. Abby was used to helping pregnant women and babies. He supposed the thought of traveling to the morgue did not appeal to her. Blake fought away the urge he had to comfort her and focused on the chief.

"What about Hancock's lawyer?" Eli asked. "Blake said that his information was on the chart."

"It's a phony. There's no lawyer—at least, not at that phone line. Just a bunch of numbers and a phony name someone keyed in."

"And who did key in all of that information at Fairview? Who placed my name with Hancock? I should never have been that man's doctor," Blake said.

"No one." McClendon shrugged. "Our computer experts tore that system apart. But they cannot find where, when or who keyed in Hancock's information and none of the data-entry personnel would own up to having done it."

"Anything else?" Blake asked, still waiting for McClendon's big accusation toward him.

The chief looked across the table at him. "Perhaps you would prefer to speak in private, Dr. Jamison?"

Blake shrugged. He felt Abby's eyes on him. He didn't like the tense expression on her face. No, he wasn't going to speak in private. He had nothing to do with Hancock. Of that he was certain. And he had nothing to hide from Abby or her family. "Thank you. But I don't see any reason for that."

"Good." The chief looked pleased, which gave Blake some relief. Maybe what he had to say wasn't so bad after all.

McClendon took out a file folder and placed it in the center of the table, opened it and spread the pages out. "This is Hancock's file. Here we see your name, Dr. Jamison. And your signature. Here is the lawyer's contact info. But this…this is the doctor who transferred Hancock to Fairview. Here are the insurance papers explaining the need for transfer. Everything is in order. Dr. Jamison, is there anything in the chart you'd like to explain to us?"

Blake clenched his teeth. He didn't like the way the chief was looking at him. He picked up the file and scanned through it. "There's more information here than what I saw yesterday. A complete workup of his surgery."

"Like I said, Dr. Dodd apologized for that. This is a complete and accurate file."

"Oh, and this!" Blake couldn't hide the surprise in his voice. "The name of the physician who transferred Hancock to Fairview." He reread the file in disbelief. He knew the name. He knew the name very well. "Dr. Granger. He was a friend of my parents'. A very good friend, actually."

"I know, Dr. Jamison," the chief said. "On a hunch, since the patient and one of our key witnesses were both from New York, I ran some searches through newspaper articles to see if there was any connection between you and Hancock. I didn't find one—until I searched for ties between you and Hancock's doctor. Then the screen lit up with hits of articles and pictures of Dr. Granger and your parents at one society event after another. I also discovered that you're now worth a lot of money since the loss of your parents. I don't believe in coincidence. You just arrived and we have a murder in the hospital, which is connected back to someone you know in New York. Why don't you tell us exactly why you came to Lancaster so we can all get to the bottom of this?"

Blake nodded. "Right. I'd be glad to, actually. It's time everyone knew...."

"So, that's your family connection in Lancaster?" Abby said. "You're looking for your birth parents? That's kind of a big deal."

"Yes." Blake nodded. "After mulling it over for several months, I decided it's the right thing to do."

Abby stood, trying to think of how to respond. It was difficult to concentrate with everything she had on her mind. Hannah, her brother and Chief McClendon had already left the kitchen. Before leaving, the chief had given them an hour to get to the morgue and make the ID on Hancock's body. Abby was dreading that. She didn't want to look at a dead body. She didn't want to think about the man on the gurney, whom she'd seen murdered. It was enough that she saw him all the time in her mind. And his killer with his cold eyes.

So far, this was not the day she'd hoped for. The only thing that would make it worse would be running into her father. She did not have the energy or the heart for that.

"You don't approve of me looking for my birth parents, do you? What if I told you my mother believed that my parents were Amish?" Blake looked at her with his soft brown eyes. He wanted her approval. She wondered why. She hardly knew him.

"It's none of my business, Blake…but Amish? Are you sure?"

"Well, no. I'm not sure about any of it, except that I'm adopted. I only know what my mother said in her letter."

Abby had a million things she wanted to say, but she shook them off. It was truly none of her business. "Shall we go, then? I really want to get out of here before my father arrives."

"Sure." He looked disappointed that she didn't want to discuss his search for his birth parents.

"I'll just fetch my bag." She headed for the steps. "I'll meet you outside."

Abby grabbed her things and headed back to the living room. But she hadn't been fast enough. She slowed her descent as she saw *Dat* waiting at the bottom of the stairs. It was the first time she'd seen him since telling him about her decision not to join the church. It seemed in those two long weeks that he'd noticeably aged. The creases around his mouth and eyes were more pronounced. His hair thinner. His shoulders more rounded. Or was that her guilt making her see him in that way?

"Hello, *Dat*. How are you?"

The bishop took one look at her fitted jeans and sweater, letting out a disapproving huff as he ran his hands up and down his suspenders in an agitated motion. He readjusted his straw hat and tugged at his long, white beard.

"You should have tried all of this during your *Rumschpringe*. That's what run-around time is for. You were supposed to get all of this—" he motioned to her clothing "—out of your system. And now look what is happening. The outside world is crashing down around you, collapsing. And you are going down with it. I knew this would happen. And I knew how painful it would be to watch."

"You knew about what?"

"I can see the police car. I know what it means. I have heard the reports from the hospital and the Youngers. There has been a murder, and you have brought the killer into our world. What if that man had hurt that little boy?"

"And that would be my fault? I saw a doctor kill a patient. I am responsible for my own actions. Not for those of others. Isn't that what you always preach?" Abby had been completely wrong in thinking her father would be upset with Eli for bringing the police to the house. The bishop's anger was all directed at her. And if there was anything that made Abby down, it was disappointing her father. Even as she tried to defend herself and her actions, her head dropped.

"*Dat,* this is nothing. I was just in the wrong place at the wrong time. Chief McClendon will clear this all up in no time. You don't need to worry."

"Exactly. Wrong place. You do not belong there in that hospital. And now you are running around with this doctor?" He crossed his arms over his chest.

"I'm not running around with anyone. He saved my life, *Dat.* Twice. He's just giving me a ride back to the hospital so I can get my car." *And ID the man I saw murdered.* She decided to leave that part out.

"What do you know about this *Englischer?* He looks very worldly. I saw that fancy car of his."

Abby knew she was never going to win this discussion, not today, anyway. She might as well give up on it and talk about something productive. Her mind turned back to Blake's story.

She reached for her father's hand. He was a good man. A good father. A good bishop. He was wise, even if she felt he was a bit blinded when it came to looking at her situation. She took in a deep breath and smiled at him.

"What's that look for?" he asked. "I know that look. You're up to something. Abigail?"

If anyone would know about Amish adoptions, it would be her father. "*Dat,* let's not argue today. Let's just pray for everyone's safety and for a quick resolution to this situation and then we can pick this back up later. Okay?"

He grumbled but gave her hand a squeeze.

"So, I have a question for you. Have you ever heard of an Amish couple giving up a child for adoption?"

"Why do you ask this?" He frowned. "One of your patients wants to give up a child? This needs much prayer."

"So, it does happen?"

"There have been some times when a family could not keep a child. But always that child goes to another Amish family. Always. Why do you ask? I can see you are thinking something serious."

"No. Not really, *Dat,*" Abby said. "This has to do with the doctor. He was adopted and wants to find his birth parents. He thinks they might be Amish."

"See? You are attached to this doctor. I told you." Her father's expression darkened. "No, this story of his cannot be true. Amish do not give away children. We take care of our own. You tell your doctor friend to go back to his real home. He can only cause heartache here if he tries to dig for fool's gold."

"That's what I thought, too." Abby smiled and patted her father on the shoulder. "See, *Dat?* We still agree about most things. Don't worry about me."

"*Ach.* How can I not worry? My daughter. A car. A job. Police. You should be married. Cooking. Taking care of a family." With each word, his tone became increasingly aggravated. "What did I do wrong?"

"You didn't do anything wrong. You did everything just right." Abby kissed his cheek and headed for the door.

"Abigail." Her father's soft voice caused her to pause in the doorway. "Promise me you will not get involved with this *Englischer*. A New York man dies right after a New York doctor comes to town? You agree that it seems strange, *ja?* I do not believe in coincidences. There is more to his involvement in this affair than you think."

Abby swallowed hard, staring back at her father, whose big, kind blue eyes were focused on her with all the love of an adoring father. She'd already broken his heart and she could barely stand how that felt to her. She hadn't wanted her own decisions to cause pain to her family. Had she only been selfish in doing what she had done?

It's not too late to change your mind about joining the church, his eyes seemed to say. She couldn't ease that pain for him—but she could give him this promise.

"Do not worry about that. I can promise you with every amount of certainty that I will never get involved—as you put it—with that *Englischer*." Abby kissed his cheek, then turned and fled through the door.

Blake shifted his weight in the driver's seat of his car. He couldn't get comfortable. Abby seemed strangely preoccupied and distant after her talk with her father. "You don't approve, do you?"

"Approve of what?"

"Of the reason I came to Lancaster. To look up my birth parents."

"I don't know what I think."

"You know I wanted to tell you yesterday," Blake said. He didn't like Abby so stiff and standoffish. He felt as if he needed to explain himself. He wanted her back the way she was. So confident and natural. She had totally clammed up and he didn't know why.

"Tell me what?"

"About being adopted. I just, well...with everything that happened... And the truth is, I hadn't told anyone yet. My friends back home wouldn't know what to say. I didn't tell any of them."

"Not sure I'd know what to say, either." Abby feigned a smile. "So, I do have a question, though.... Why did the chief say that you're worth a lot of money? I'm not sure I understand what that means or how it's relevant."

Was that what was bothering her? Not the adoption, but the money? That made sense and yet it hadn't even occurred to him. "My parents—my adoptive parents, the Jamisons—did very well. They both came from society families. Then professionally, they were high-paid doctors with an elite clientele. They made good investments. They started several charities and foundations. They left me in charge of all of them, which means I get to decide where all that money goes. A lot of people in New York were surprised about that."

"Well, who else would have been in charge of it?"

"Lawyers. My parents' partners in their medical practices—particularly for the medically related charities. There are several people who could have been left in charge of various organizations. Like Dr. Granger, even. The doctor whose name is on Hancock's file. He is very involved in one particular foundation that helps underprivileged children with operable birth defects. And there are others, too. It puts me in high demand. I feel really guilty saying this but it's awfully nice to get away."

"Is that why you get so many phone calls?"

"Yes, everyone needs me to get money. You might not

have noticed but I left the phone in the car at your brother's. I didn't want to risk getting reprimanded by Hannah again."

Finally, he got a smile from her. "Do you enjoy all that work?"

"I don't know. My parents left it to me, so I feel like I need to do a good job. The charities help a lot of people. I don't want to see that fall apart. I have a responsibility to see it through."

"But do you like it? The work?"

Blake paused. "No one's ever asked me that. I don't know. I just do it. I guess I never thought about whether or not I liked it."

"Well, I love my work. I love being a nurse. I love my clinic." Abby relaxed a little, but then frowned again. He could see another question forming in her quick mind. "So why did you come here for so long? Aren't you needed back home? You could have searched for your relatives from New York. Right?"

Blake shrugged. That was a good question. But he wasn't ready to answer it. He didn't know the reason himself. "Seemed like I should do it myself, in person."

Abby sucked in a big breath.

"Are you nervous about the ID or do you have something to say?"

"Something to say." She laughed. "Guess I'm not too good at hiding my feelings."

"Say it," Blake said. "I really don't have anything to hide, despite how McClendon made it look. And I'm open to anything you want to tell me." As he spoke, he realized that that was the first time he'd ever said that to anyone.

"Well, okay, then…it's just that I don't see how your real parents could be Amish. You very well could have been born here in Lancaster. In Willow Trace even, but it's very unlikely that your parents are Amish."

He nodded, carefully watching her suspicious expressions. "You may be right, but my mother's letter says they were. You don't believe her?"

"I'm sure your mother told you what she knew. It's just that…"

"It's just that what?"

"Well, it's unlikely that an Amish couple would give up a child. Especially a son. Having sons means having farm help and labor for most families. Not to mention, every Amish church pools together an emergency fund that helps any families in need. We take care of our own. If an Amish family wanted to keep a child, everyone in the community would do anything they could to make that happen. And if that wasn't possible, they'd settle the baby with another Amish family."

He looked down, taking in her logic. "I didn't know that."

"And it's not merely that. It's also the impact your search might have on the people you're searching for."

"How do you mean?" Blake wanted to hear her thoughts. Having been raised Amish, she would have much more insight into the effects of his family connections.

"Well, can you imagine? You have the trauma of giving up a child and never thinking you'll see him again. If that child came back, it would bring up those emotions and hurt all over again. Not to mention the effect it would have on other family members. This isn't a small thing you are talking about. It's an event that would change many people's lives. Not just your own."

She touched his hand softly. The contact sent all sorts of feeling rushing through him. He thought of her words and her wisdom.

"This is important to you, isn't it?" Her voice was soft.

"I'm sorry. It's really none of my business. I shouldn't have said anything. I didn't mean to upset you."

Blake swallowed hard, pulling his hand away from her. What if Abby was right? What if his one clue to track down his parents wasn't true? The thought left Blake feeling hollow inside. "It is important to me. I wasn't sure how I felt about it at first. But now that I'm here, I really want to know. I want to know if I'm from here."

He looked out the windshield at the beautiful rolling hills, the draping evergreens and the scattered farmhouses. It felt like home to him. A lifetime of living in the city and one trip to Lancaster and this—this rural country-side he'd never seen before felt like home. Either he was imagining the calm comfort he felt inside or this land was in his bones.

"What about McClendon's suspicions that your decision to come here started all this mess?"

Abby's direct question shook him from his daydreams of home and family. "Should I take it from your tone that it's now your suspicion, too?"

"Well, it does seem coincidental. Too coincidental. Your name mysteriously appearing on the chart? The former doctor being a friend of the family?"

What was she thinking? Blake lowered his brows. "You think I dosed Hancock? Or let him die?"

Abby looked at him as if he'd grown two heads. "No. Of course not. If I thought that I wouldn't be in this car with you. I'm just saying that... Well, I don't know what I'm saying. I just want to make sense of all of this. And it doesn't make sense, does it?"

Blake shook his head. "No, it doesn't. And I want to make sense of it, too."

He parked in front of the hospital in the convenient physicians' parking. They walked inside and headed down to the morgue. The pit-bull detective, Langer, was waiting for them.

"One at a time. And no commenting to each other in between viewings."

Abby went first. It didn't take but a couple of minutes and she was back out. She didn't even look at Blake as she passed. He followed Langer in. The autopsist stood by a table with a body lying on it, covered with a sheet. Langer nodded to the other doctor, who lifted back the sheet, revealing the face of the body. Short, bald, olive skin.

Blake nodded. "Yep. That's…that's Hancock."

SEVEN

You cannot serve both God and the world, Abigail. Her father's words echoed through her head. *What do you know about this* Englischer?

She glanced over at Blake. He was bent over her clinic floor, sweeping the last bit of glass into a dustpan. They had been working on her messy clinic ever since they'd left the morgue.

Her father had been right. She didn't know much about Dr. Blake Jamison. It seemed the more she learned about him the more confused it all became.

"Thanks for helping," she said. "I'm sure you have something else you'd rather be doing."

"Not really." Blake dumped the rest of the glass into the trash. "I'm glad to help. Like I said, it's nice to get my mind off things."

"So, what have you done in searching for your parents?"

He narrowed his eyes at her in a playful manner. "You sure you want to know?"

"I asked."

"Well, I went out early this morning to the lawyer's office—the lawyer who supposedly handled my adoption, according to my mother and the paperwork her lawyer compiled." Blake crossed his arms over his chest. She couldn't help but notice the muscular definition of his arms under his rolled-up sleeves, or the way his skin was sprinkled with freckles. "The receptionist really gave me the runaround. Told me I had the wrong lawyer. She wouldn't even let me speak to Mr. Linton. It was very strange."

"So, what now?"

"I can't imagine why, but I'm almost certain she was lying to me. So, I left a message for Mr. Pooler, my mother's lawyer back in New York, to see if there is anything he can do or suggest to me. I'm hoping he calls me back this afternoon."

"Well, don't be too discouraged even if he doesn't. There are other ways to find your birth parents."

Blake gave her a long, sideways look. "I thought you didn't approve of my quest. Now more questions and suggestions?"

"Well, if you don't want to hear it…" She started to walk away.

"No, no. I do. I value your opinion."

"You know, just because we are different and don't agree about this doesn't mean I can't be helpful." She finished arranging her supplies and leaned her weight over the counter, letting his compliment wash over her.

He leaned toward her. Was he flirting? She backed away, remembering her promise to her father. Even if she were attracted to Blake, which she wasn't, she would never go back on that promise. She'd broken her father's heart once. She wouldn't do it again. Anyway, it wasn't even an issue because she hardly even liked him and they had nothing in common. Nothing at all to worry about.

"Actually, while you were talking to your dad, Eli told me that he could help me get into the town hall and gain access to the public birth records there." He stood back again as if suddenly aware that he'd entered her personal space. His freckled cheeks flushed. "I think I might take him up on that."

"Eli can be very resourceful when it comes to getting information." She motioned toward the kitchen. "I don't know about you, but I'm starving. Want to join me for a sandwich? It's the least I can do after all your help. I had no idea it would take so long."

"Sounds great."

She led him to the kitchen, where just the night before they'd seen an intruder.

"What can I do to help?"

Abby thought for a second, then headed to the refrigerator. "You can sit down and tell me what you like on your sandwich."

"The works." Blake pulled his cell phone from his back pocket and placed it on the kitchen table as he took a seat.

"Phone's been quiet today," Abby commented as she grabbed condiments, sliced honey ham, lettuce, pickles and tomatoes.

Almost as soon as the words were said, his cell began to vibrate on the table. Her eyes gravitated to the large image on its big touch screen—the very clear image of a lovely, sophisticated brunette. The name *Natalie* flashed across the top. Blake picked up the device quickly. Too quickly. "Oh, no. You spoke too soon. Excuse me."

"Of course." She turned back to the counter quickly, feeling as if she'd imposed on his privacy. Of course Blake had a girlfriend. What did she care?

She shook her head. She was only glad her father wasn't there.

"Hello." Why had he grabbed the phone so quickly and stepped out of the kitchen as if he'd needed serious privacy to talk to Natalie? He had no idea—he only wished he hadn't done it. Not that Abigail would care. She was not interested in him as anything more than a friend, but it still gave the wrong impression. It made it seem as if he had something to hide from her when in reality, she was the one person he felt completely comfortable telling the truth.

"Blake!" Natalie's voice was cheerful but guarded. "I—I was just going to leave you a message to remind you of the fund-raising gala next weekend. I hope you're still going to be my date."

"Look, Nat. I'm still in Pennsylvania and in the middle of something. I can't—"

"You're not canceling on me, are you?"

Yes, he wanted to say. But how could he miss the gala? It was a fund-raiser for one of his parents' charities. Didn't he owe it to their memory to attend? And anyway, it was still several days away. This mess with Hancock and the lawyer's strange behavior might be completely resolved by then. "Things here are a little up in the air—I don't know when I'll be getting back to town. I'll call you later. Can't talk right now. Goodbye, Natalie.

"I don't know why I walked out of the room to take that," he said as he reentered the kitchen.

"None of my business." Abby put their sandwiches on the table, turned and smiled at him. "Anyway, no one likes to blab in front of others on a cell phone."

Her nonchalant attitude stung. Clearly she couldn't have cared less about whom he was talking to on the phone.

Blake looked down hungrily at the food but waited as he noticed Abby did not eat.

"Would you mind if I said grace?"

"Of course not."

Abby bowed her head. "Dear Father, thank You for providing this meal for us. Thank You for Your hand upon us, which has kept us safe. Thank You for new friends and the blessing of a helping hand. Amen."

"Amen," he repeated. That was two days in a row now he had prayed, after so long a hiatus. The feeling it brought him was sharp and pricked right at his heart.

"Are you a praying man, Blake?"

"Why? Do I look awkward about it?" He tried to laugh as if his words were meant as a joke. Abby's face showed that her answer, if she had answered, would have been in the affirmative. "Yes, I am," he clarified. "It's just been a while."

"You should change that."

"I think I should change a lot of things in my life."

Blake felt as if he could talk to Abby about anything. He had the strongest urge to reach out and touch her long, silky hair. He wanted to know what it would feel like in his fingers. But he could see in her interactions with him that she did not feel that way about him. He needed to push away his silly and fruitless thoughts.

It was for the best that she wasn't interested in him as anything but a friend. The last thing he needed was to get attached to someone right now. His life was a wreck. He could barely handle things as they were. But then why did he feel so relaxed and content here and at the Millers' and working alongside Abby in the clinic?

"So you live here alone? No boyfriend? No husband?" he teased. "You said that was a common topic around here, so I thought I'd bring it up again."

His words caused her to blush. "No. I courted some here and there. Mostly Amish men. A few *Englischers*. Nothing serious. I'm not interested in marriage. I just want to run my clinic and help people. It's my calling in life and I feel God wants me to be 100 percent devoted to it. If I marry and have a family, I can't give 100 percent. But I haven't always been alone here. I did have a roommate for a while. A young girl from Philadelphia. She's at college now."

Not interested in marriage? Blake was stunned. And if he was really honest with himself, he was a little bit disappointed, too. He'd not thought of Abby as the career-driven type. But all the more reason to keep it professional between the two of them.

After they finished, Abby snatched up both the plates with a grin and headed to the sink.

"Let me help." His hand brushed against hers as she passed with the plates.

"You've done more than your fair share of cleaning up around here. And I have really appreciated it."

Blake started to respond but once again his cell phone vibrated. "It's Pooler, the lawyer. Do you mind?"

She shook her head and smiled.

The lawyer that looked so much like Linton.... Blake found himself wondering just how much he should share with Pooler. His gut seemed to tell him to trust the man as little as possible.

After a quick phone call, Blake came back into the kitchen with a look of hope on his face. "Can you believe my lawyer was able to get ahold of Mr. Linton and set up a real meeting for this afternoon? Apparently, the brush-off I got before was just because the receptionist doesn't take too kindly to walk-ins."

"That's good news for you." So why did Abby get a sinking feeling about Blake's plans? After all, it was none of her business. "So, just like that you could find out the names of your real parents? That must be a strange thought."

"Yes. Hard to believe, really." He smiled. "I have to take

off, though. If I rush, I'll just make it. The office is all the way in Millersville."

"Well, you'd better get going. Thanks again for your help today, Blake. I guess I'll see you next time McClendon calls us together or at the hospital sometime." It felt strange to Abby to be saying goodbye to Blake after all the intensity of being with him over the past day and a half.

"Thanks for lunch." He started toward the front door and she followed him to see him out. "You should think about a security system."

"You sound like Eli." She laughed. "Truth is, I can't afford one. I don't charge most of my patients and I only work part-time at the hospital, so things are a little tight."

"You don't charge your patients?"

"Not money—not if they can't afford it. Sometimes they pay cash. If not, they pay me in other ways. Food, usually. I've gotten a few quilts. One couple whose twins I delivered brought me a pig."

"So, you buy all this medicine and these supplies out of your own pocket?" He looked incredulous, as if he'd never heard of such a thing.

"Haven't you ever worked at a free clinic? Or offered your services to the poor?"

"Well, yes, but only once or twice a year. Not every day. You are full of surprises, Abigail."

Abby wasn't sure if he meant it as a compliment or if he found her way of life ludicrous. It was obvious he was rich and was used to a completely different way of life, but yesterday during the entire trauma, she'd thought him a little deeper than this. Perhaps he wasn't? Perhaps he was *Hochmut* through and through.

He stopped again at the door.

"Did you forget something?"

"Well, yes, I sort of forgot about being your doctor."

He turned and looked at her head wound. "It's healing up really nicely but..."

"But what?"

"I have to advise against driving alone the day after you had a concussion."

Abby smiled. "But I already drove from the hospital to here."

"I know, but I was following you. I should follow you back to Eli's. You are staying there tonight, right?"

Abby nodded. "Quit worrying. You can't miss your appointment. Go on. I'll be fine. I'm only driving to Eli's and you know that's not too far."

Blake hesitated. "I don't know, Abby. You have been doing well, but you must be exhausted. I can reschedule my appointment. I'm not even sure if you should be alone. Not after all the things that have been happening."

"Bye, Blake." Abby practically pushed him out the door. Maybe it wasn't so smart to be alone. But she needed it. Her head was spinning, her feelings flying. She had patients to check on. And she had information she wanted to look up. She wanted Blake gone to be able to do it.

Clouds descended over the Lancaster skies as Blake drove back to the lawyer's office. Looked as if a big winter storm was blowing in or over. With all that was going on, he'd hardly thought to check the weather. A bad feeling chilled him as he reached the little village of Millersville. He still didn't feel right about leaving Abby alone. He should have followed her to her brother's. After all, she'd had a concussion the day before.

Meanwhile, he also kept thinking about what the others suspected—that his arrival in Lancaster had sparked this awful chain of events. He had come to Lancaster to find his birth parents—could his quest be connected to Hancock in some way?

And what about Dr. Granger? Blake hadn't heard from him in months, not since his parents' funeral. Dr. Granger had always been such a close friend of his parents'. Almost a part of the family. Blake assumed McClendon's detectives had made contact with him, but he could, too. He wanted to hear about the transfer and hopefully get some more information on the patient. Blake slid his cell from his pocket. At the next stoplight, he thumbed through his contacts and dialed Dr. Frank Granger.

"Dr. Granger's office. How may I direct your call?" A polite young voice sounded on the line.

"Hi. This is Blake Jamison. I'm a family friend of Dr. Granger's. I'd like to speak with him or leave a voice mail if I could."

There was a long hesitation before the receptionist said, "Dr. Granger is out on vacation this week. I'm taking messages but he will not return any calls until he is back in the States."

Blake swallowed hard. This was most unexpected. How could Granger have transferred a patient just yesterday if he were on vacation? "When did the doctor leave?"

"Over a week ago."

"And he returns soon?"

"He'll be back from St. Thomas midweek."

"Thank you. I'll call back."

Blake threw his phone aside as he turned his car into the same office-building strip he'd visited early that morning. He drove to the center of the parking lot and hit the brakes. There was the dental office that he'd seen on the left and there was the dermatologist's office to the right. But where Linton's office had been, there was nothing. The shades that had been in the windows and the sign with Linton's name—they were all gone. The office was empty, as if nothing had ever been there.

Blake parked his Land Rover in an empty space right in front. He hopped out of his car and raced up to the front door of the office. As he had expected, the rooms inside were empty. There was no reception desk. No large wing-backed chairs to wait in. Even the wall paintings were gone. There was nothing left but the carpet. So, how had Mr. Pooler just been on the phone with Linton not even an hour ago? It would have taken half the day to move out all of the fancy furnishings from inside the plush office—and it would have taken planning in advance to hire the movers. Yet there had been no signs of a planned move when he'd arrived earlier. It was as if the whole thing had been staged. But Linton couldn't have possibly known he was coming that morning. Only Pooler had known that....

Blake turned around, facing the parking lot. He blew out a long sigh of serious frustration. Maybe Abigail was right. Maybe searching for his birth parents was a bad idea. He'd certainly thought it would be a much easier endeavor than it had turned out to be thus far.

What should I do, Lord?

He raised his question hesitantly to the sky. Prayer had become awkward. How had that happened? A flake of snow flittered down from the sky as Blake looked out over the empty lot.

Zing. Something hot and fast and small grazed by his forehead. A second later the glass doors behind him shattered into a million bits that scattered over the sidewalk. Blake dropped to the ground, pressing his back flat against the grill of his car. That had been a bullet. Someone was shooting at him.

EIGHT

Whew. Abby closed the door behind Blake. She was glad for a moment to catch her breath and think on her own. She had told Hannah she'd be back at five o'clock. And she did need to return before Eli started to worry. She didn't want him calling Chief McClendon again. Or worse, her father.

She checked the time—she had just enough to feed the animals and call a few patients. First, Mrs. Brenneman. Abby dialed the number of the prepaid cell phone that she'd given to them. She often did that for her patients who owned oil-powered generators that could keep the phones charged when it was close to their due date. That way it would be easy for them to get in touch with her when it was time.

"Hello, Anna? This is Abigail Miller. I'm sorry I didn't get a chance to visit you yesterday."

"Ja." Anna's voice sounded over the line. "We have heard that you had an accident. Are you okay?"

"I'm fine. The real question is, how are you feeling?"

"I'm tired. A little pain in my side," she said. "It won't be long now."

"It's still a little early, Anna. How much work are you doing?"

"Not so much."

"None. No more work. You need at least one more week. Keep your phone close by at all times and call me right away if you have more pain."

"*Ja,* okay."

Abby was worried about Anna. She wasn't sure if the woman realized the dangers to the baby if he or she came too early. But it was hard to get an Amish woman to leave the chores for others to handle.

Next, she called Becka Esche. Her baby was also due anytime now, and it had been a rough pregnancy even though she was young and it was her second. Abby had insisted a few times that Becka see a doctor. But sometimes there was only so much Abby could convince her patients to do. Becka had delivered her first child in the hospital with an *Englisch* doctor. She'd lost the baby just hours after delivery, while she herself had developed a very dangerous condition called placenta accreta that nearly killed her. Now she and her husband, Jonas, wanted nothing to do with the hospital or any *Englisch* doctors. Abby could hardly blame them.

"Becka? This is Abigail. How are you feeling?"

"Ready to have this baby," she said. "I think it's almost time."

"Yes, it will be soon. Get lots of rest. Keep your phone close by."

Abby had other patients, of course. But none she needed to contact at the moment. That done, she fed her animals, collected her things and headed to Eli's. It was getting late, and as nice as it was to pretend everything was fine, she knew she needed to get back to the cover of her brother's home.

As she drove along the single-lane highway, Abby realized how tired she was. Blake had been right about her exhaustion. Tonight she would fix the chamomile tea that had a natural sleep aid in it. Then she would sleep like a baby. For now, she concentrated on the road. Thankfully, it was not a long drive, even if it was down a narrow, hilly, country highway.

After a few miles, a dark sedan with very bright headlights pulled up close to the back of her car. She checked her speed. It was fine. Some people were just so impatient. But there was nowhere to pass on this narrow road and no shoulder. The hurried driver behind her would just have to wait until she turned off at Eli's place. It wasn't far now.

But the car stuck to her like glue. The driver flashed his lights even brighter and swerved his car erratically from one side of the lane to the other. Abby accelerated to put some distance between them. She hated to go over the speed limit but she feared that the driver behind her might be intoxicated and dangerous.

The sedan kept right with her. Maybe he was even closer. Abby's heart began to pound. She wanted to pull off somewhere and let him pass. But there was nowhere to turn until she came to Eli's road. Thankfully, she was almost there. If only she had hands-free calling, she could notify the police about the reckless driving. But she didn't dare take her hands from the steering wheel or her eyes from the road. It was tough enough just concentrating on keeping ahead of the crazy driver behind her.

Something wet touched her windshield. Then another something. Abby's eyes darted up to the sky. It was snowing. Great. She tapped her brakes and turned on the wipers. The sedan seemed to have fallen back a bit.

Thank goodness! Abby let out a sigh of relief.

Finally, she was near the turnoff for Eli's place. The snow was really falling now. She slowed again and suddenly there was the black sedan. It had raced up behind her, accelerating as it approached. It was so close.

Then its front bumper struck the back of Abby's car.

The force of it thrust her head into the steering wheel. The pain under normal circumstances would have been excruciating, but for Abby, with her head still tender from her attack, the agony was nearly crippling. A warm trickle of blood dribbled down her cheek, distracting her as she tried to concentrate on the road.

She held her throbbing head up and gripped the steering wheel with all her might. The road before her seemed to split in two. Abby blinked hard and tried to force her eyes to focus. But it was no use. Panic raced through her veins. In her blurry peripheral vision, the dark sedan appeared to be beside her. But Abby did not trust her double vision and she dared not take her eyes from the road in front of her to look over and check.

If she could just make it another half mile, she would be at the turnoff for Eli's farm. But as the sound of metal on metal rang in her ears, she knew she wasn't going to make it to her brother's.

Abby fought the force of the sedan against her car as best she could, keeping her steering wheel to the left as the other car pushed her to the right. Her little Malibu was no match for the big sedan and it was only seconds before her tires were sliding into the deep ditch beside the road.

No. She definitely wasn't going to make it to Eli's.

Blake's instinct was to get up and run after whoever had fired that shot, but common sense told him he'd live longer if he stayed put. He looked both ways up and down the sidewalk, his back still pressed against the front of his car. His mind felt as scattered as the shards of glass spread around him. Why was someone shooting at *him?* Everyone had thought Abby was the target....

Abby! He'd left her alone. How stupid. He needed to get

back to her as soon as possible. If someone was shooting at him, then who knew what was happening to her? His heart pounded. The shooter was behind him. Behind his car. But how far away? Blake didn't know but he would just have to risk exposing himself. He had to get into his car and head back to Abby's.

Blake stayed low and slipped back into the driver's side of his car. Starting up the car in a hurry, he floored the accelerator and raced out of the parking lot. He didn't look left or right. If the shooter was nearby, taking aim again, then so be it. He didn't care. He just had to get to Abby. He prayed he hadn't made a fatal mistake in leaving her alone.

The light snow seemed to have cleared the other drivers off the roads. He made good time back to her small cottage-clinic. But her car was already gone. Perhaps that was a good sign. He hoped that meant she was already safe at her brother's. Like she'd said earlier, it wasn't far. But he had to know for certain.

Blake pulled out his cell phone and dialed Abigail's number, which he'd programmed in earlier that morning. There was no answer. Perhaps she had the ringer off or just didn't feel like talking to him? Blake's gut told him that was not the case. Blake felt certain something was wrong. Or at least, he felt certain that he had to make sure she was all right. He would have to drive to Eli's and find out.

Blake continued on toward Eli's but much more slowly—the snow was falling harder here. He passed a car that had slipped from the increasingly icy road. Thankfully, another Good Samaritan had stopped to help the stranded driver. The closer he got to Eli's, the heavier the snow seemed to be.

Just two more curves down the winding single-lane highway, past the Youngers' bed-and-breakfast and on to Eli's farm. When he knew he was close to the hidden turnoff, Blake scouted for the difficult-to-find gravel lane. At last he saw the drive and the mailbox that read E. Miller just ahead to the left of the road. He was moving at a snail's pace now and feeling his heart sink to his stomach as he realized that in the ditch across the street from Eli's mailbox was another stranded car.

It looked abandoned. Maybe the driver had already been picked up. Blake slowed his SUV, looking closely at the vehicle in the ditch. The car was a white Chevy Malibu.

It was Abby's car and she was still inside.

Oh, Lord, please, please let her be alive....

NINE

What had he done by leaving her alone?

It was immediately obvious that she had been attacked. The back bumper was dented and scratched, as was the driver's-side door. This was no accident— another vehicle had pushed her off the road. And the car hadn't been abandoned, either. Abby was still inside. Blake could just see the top of her head. She wasn't moving. A rush of frantic alarm hit him hard in the gut.

He threw his car into Park and raced across the street to the ditch. Based on the amount of snow on the car, she had not been there long. The engine was still hot and had melted everything touching the hood. Blake swiped the thin layer of flakes from the window so that he had a better view inside. Abby's body lay back against her seat. Her head was slumped forward in an awkward position. But he could see a mark across her forehead from the steering wheel. There was blood and dust from the air bag on her skin. "Abby!" He pulled at the door handle but it wouldn't open. "Abby! Wake up! Come on!"

Was she unconscious or was she…? Fear seized his body and mind. For a quick instant, he himself felt paralyzed. Then he rapped on the glass. Abby did not move. Blake knocked harder, then pounded on the glass with his fist. Abby did not respond.

Be alive! Please, God, let her be alive.

Blake searched the ditch. Just under and behind the car, he found a large stone. He stepped away from the backseat window and threw the stone like a cannon through the glass.

It cracked into a million pieces but did not shatter. Blake removed his jacket and covered his right hand. He picked up the stone again and pushed it through the weakest point in the break. Shards of glass scattered over the backseat. He reached inside, keeping the jacket around his arm to protect himself as he leaned forward and unlocked the driver's door.

Throwing the jacket aside, he opened Abby's door. His fingers went straight to the tender spot just under the neck as he felt for her pulse. Her body was warm, and with great relief, he detected the lightest rhythm of blood flow. He watched the rise and fall of her chest. She was alive.

Thank You, God...

Abby floated in a delightful dream. Cold air blew on her cheeks. Her hair was loose and flowing. Tiny icy dewdrops kissed her face and neck. It felt lovely. She drifted, flew, glided over a field of white tulips. The tall, handsome doctor stood at the edge of the flowers, watching her. He smiled and she laughed as a blast of cold air blew her nearer to him. His arms reached out and held her. They were warm and strong as he whispered to her. But she could not understand his words and then he was gone.

Darkness overcame her and she felt a hand on her arm. She turned back to see that a man in scrubs held her. He was tall and round and breathed heavily, like an old man. His eyes were gray and glassy. He pulled down his surgi-

*cal mask and whispered her name as if he knew her well.
Her arm ached. He pulled her back, then thrust her forward. She hit something hard and sharp. Her whole head
filled with pain—incredible pain. If she could just open
her eyes again... But she could not.*

*The dream faded as the throbbing in her head in-
creased. She was sleepy and she longed to hear Blake's
voice again.*

Blake placed Abby gently into the backseat of his car.
He had not called 9-1-1. Abby had responded to his touch
with just enough movement to give him hope that her injuries didn't require immediate paramedic care. She had
no broken bones. He'd checked for that. So there really
wasn't much point in an emergency crew driving her on
icy roads. Anyway, he was a doctor—and a pretty good
one. He would take care of her.

He drove slowly up the winding gravel drive, spotting
Eli near the front of the stables. Hearing the car, Eli waved
to him, the friendly greeting adding to the guilt Blake felt
at having allowed Abby to drive alone. Eli would blame
him, too. And Abby, too, once she woke up.

"Abby's been in a car accident," Blake called to Eli as
he stepped out of his SUV.

Eli dropped what he was doing and ran over. "Where
is she?"

"Here." Blake motioned to his backseat. "I was wondering if you'd help me take her inside."

"*Ja,* of course. Or does she need to go to the hospital?
She is so pale."

Blake looked over Abby again. He crouched down to
lift her from his car. She stirred slightly for the first time,
her eyelids fluttering. "I think she's coming to. If you'll
allow me, I could examine her inside and we can make her

comfortable. There is nothing broken that I can tell. And if the head swelling looks okay and she isn't bleeding too badly, I think the hospital can wait. It might be more dangerous driving in the storm."

Eli nodded. "Where was the accident?"

"Just in front of your drive. On the main road. Looked like another vehicle forced her off the road. We need to call Chief McClendon. There should be an investigation."

"And you were behind her?" Eli kept his eyes glued to his sister as Blake made his way with her across the porch and into the living room.

"No." Blake kneeled as he laid Abby carefully on the couch. He placed a pillow under her head and looked over her head wound again. He didn't want to tell Eli that he'd let her drive alone. *If only she would wake up...* "I need to wash my hands. Do you have better lighting?"

"Not really. With an oil-powered generator, which is the only power source allowed, we tend to use low-wattage bulbs. I can get a strong flashlight. We use those instead of the dangerous lanterns."

"What about ice? An ice pack would be good for her."

Eli pointed to the kitchen. "You can wash your hands there, as well. I'll stay with her and get the flashlight when you come back...but, Blake, I thought the two of you were together. I thought you weren't going to leave her alone."

"I had a meeting, so I let Abby drive over here by herself." Blake explained exactly what had happened. "I wasn't thinking."

Eli touched Blake's shoulder in a brotherly way, but Blake could feel Eli's anger. He admired the man's ability to control his first reaction. Whether it was an Amish trait or just unique to Eli, it was something he needed to work on for himself.

"We will discuss this later," Eli said.

Blake nodded and handed him his cell phone. "You should also know that someone took a shot at me while I was in Millersville. When McClendon arrives, I'll fill you in on the details. I think your sister needs protection."

"Sounds like you both do," Eli said as he took the phone. Blake headed to the kitchen to clean his hands and get ice and try to calm his rattled nerves.

"I hit my head two days in a row? I can't believe it." Abby tried to sit up but immediately gave up the idea as a debilitating wave of pain traveled from her temples to the back of her skull and around again. "Ugh. Okay, I believe it."

"You should have taken some of the Motrin the doctor tried to give you." Hannah fluffed up the pillows behind her.

"Doctor?" She glanced at Eli, who'd been talking to her for the past twenty minutes, helping her remember the car accident with the big black sedan in the snow. "I thought that was Chief McClendon here with you."

"McClendon is here and your friend Dr. Jamison," Eli said. "Blake's the one who found your car in the ditch. You were unconscious. He brought you up to the house. He and the chief are outside at the end of the drive now, looking at the damage to your car."

"Here, have some of this tea you're always making us drink." Hannah passed her a warm mug.

"I had the strangest dream." Abby wrapped her hands around the cup, lifting the strong, familiar brew to her lips.

"I guess that's normal after a concussion. Was it about the accident?" Hannah asked.

"No, it was about flowers and—" *Blake* "—and...the man who attacked me."

"Do you think the man driving the car was the man who attacked you? The man from the hospital?"

"I don't know. I couldn't really see inside the car. Plus, I was mostly concentrating on trying to stay on the road.... So, what was Blake doing out here? I thought he was going to talk to some lawyer and then head back to the bed-and-breakfast."

"He did go to the lawyer's," Eli said. "And someone shot at him. So he came racing over here to make sure you were safe."

"What? Someone shot at him? As in, with a gun?" Abby's eyes went wide. "Is he okay?"

"Let her rest, Eli. She's tired and you're getting her all excited," Hannah said. "I've made enough food for everyone. We can talk about everything that's happened at dinner."

Abby didn't like the way Eli and Hannah were coddling her and she really didn't like the way they talked about Blake, almost as if he was a family member. Good grief. They hardly knew him. And maybe it had taken getting her head hit again but she'd decided that she didn't want to know him. She didn't like the weird way she felt around him. She didn't like that she'd gotten a little bit excited when Eli had said Blake had come to check on her. And she really didn't like when his phone rang and the display showed that beautiful women were calling him. Why did she even care about any of this? She shouldn't—it was as simple as that.

"Well, is he okay? You can at least tell me that...."

Not that she cared...much.

"He's fine."

Heavy footfalls sounded on the front porch. Eli went to the front door to let Blake and the chief back into the house. Abby wanted to blend away into the sofa cushions. She could only imagine how awful she must look after being in another accident. There was blood on her sweater. Her hair had fallen out of the tight braid and she ached from head to toe. She wanted quiet. She wanted safety. She wanted to go back to her life before Blake Jamison.

But despite her thoughts, McClendon and Blake tromped into the living room looking half-frozen as they brushed away the snow from their pant legs. Blake carried her overnight bag in his arms. "Here you go. Thought you might be needing this. I couldn't help noticing your laptop is in there. Do you have internet here? Does Hannah allow that?"

He smiled as he looked at her with his soft brown eyes. Ugh. She didn't want to smile back at him, but he made it pretty hard. It was difficult to will yourself not to like someone that you were naturally drawn to—and no matter how she sliced it, she was naturally attracted to Blake Jamison.

"No internet here. I have a wireless plan. An AirCard." She put a finger over her lips to indicate it was her secret from Hannah.

But Hannah had overheard. She shook her head in disapproval before offering dinner to everyone.

McClendon declined. "Thank you, but I'll have to be going. Lots of work for the police on a snowy day. Speaking of which, the tow truck will not be coming until tomorrow. He's got other jobs that can't wait. I hope you don't mind that I told him that this one could."

"Not at all." Abby forced herself into a sitting position, shutting her eyes against the excruciating pain in her head. "I don't think I'll be going anywhere anytime soon."

Blake mumbled something about not letting her go anywhere, then turned to Eli. "I don't want to impose, but I think I should stay to keep an eye on your sister tonight. After two blows to the head, there could be complications."

Eli gave a quick nod. "You're welcome to stay. Actually, in light of this unexpected storm, I could use your help getting the animals into the barn."

"Animals? Right. Of course. Be happy to help. Just need to call the Youngers at the bed-and-breakfast and let them know I'll be staying here." He pulled out his cell phone and followed Hannah and Eli into the kitchen, leaving Abby alone with the chief.

McClendon sat on a small wooden stool close to the sofa. "Are you up for giving me a quick statement?"

Abby gave a slight nod and recounted the accident. "Unlike yesterday, I remember it perfectly, right up until the moment the air bags inflated."

"Did you get a license number?"

"No. He was always behind me."

"Could you describe the driver?"

She shook her head. "Tinted windows and it was snowing. Plus, I was keeping my eyes on the road."

McClendon showed some dissatisfaction with her response. "There's something I don't quite get."

"What's that?"

"If you came straight from your house to your brother's after Dr. Jamison left for Millersville, then how is it that your car engine was still warm when he found you after going there and all the way back?"

"I didn't come straight here." Abby looked directly at the chief. "I made some phone calls first and saw to my animals."

"Miss Miller, I hardly need remind you that you were attacked inside the hospital yesterday. I thought you understood not to—"

"I'm not sure it would have made a difference. Someone shot at Blake. Seems like whoever it is can find us wherever we go—and *when*ever we go."

"What do you know about the shooting?"

"Nothing except that it happened, and Blake is fine. Aside from that, no one told me a thing."

"Not much to tell you," Blake said from the doorway. Apparently, he'd been listening in on their conversation. His voice gave her a start. "I went back to Linton's office. It had been cleared out since this morning. Not even a scrap of paper left behind. I turned around and a shot was fired just to the side of me. I thought of you and how if someone was attacking me, they might go after you next. I couldn't believe I'd listened to you and left you alone. I jumped back into the car and raced over. A little too late. I should have never left you at the clinic."

"I didn't give you much choice," Abby said.

"*Ach.* The truth." Eli reentered the living space, too. He shook his head at her, mocking her stubborn ways. "Come on, Blake. Need to get the babies inside."

"Babies?"

"Calves. Lambs, too."

"Ah."

They were dressed for the snow, ready to tackle the evening chores. Abby wondered how Blake would manage. It was clear by the expression on his face that tending to animals was not something he was used to.

"So, Blake," Abby said as he and her brother headed to the front door, "since you've been shot at, what do you think about your involvement now? Still think it's all coincidence?"

Blake looked to McClendon. Perhaps they'd had a similar conversation outside.

He paused, then let out a long sigh. "It still doesn't fit together. It's hard to imagine that I brought this mess here. But I've never believed in coincidence."

Abby tried to nod, but her head wouldn't move as Blake's

eyes seemed to have a fast hold on her. He stepped back into the room again.

"You should know, too, that I tried to call Dr. Granger on my way to Linton's office to ask him about transferring Hancock. His administrative assistant told me that he's been out of the country for the week. So there's no way he transferred Hancock. His name was probably put into Hancock's medical file the same way mine was—and I don't think any of us believe that was a coincidence."

Blake shook his head. "I still don't understand how any of it connects to my adoption or my choice to come here to look for my birth parents. Especially since, as I told you, no one knows about that except for you. And why would anyone kill over an adoption? So that makes me think of my parents' deaths and the inheritance. Then again, it could be none of those things."

"We are working on all those angles, Dr. Jamison." McClendon stood from the stool and walked toward the two men, though he continued to face Abby. "A killer is after both of you. Probably the very one who killed Hancock. It's pretty likely he spotted you and the doctor at the hospital, followed you home and then here. And from the shooting and the timing of the car attack, it seems that there must be another person involved."

"And don't forget that one of them speaks Pennsylvania Dutch," Abby said.

McClendon nodded. "The FBI is considering all of this."

"The FBI?" Blake repeated.

"Sure. We have to involve the FBI—they are trying to identify Hancock. Taking fingerprints and running them as we speak."

Eli checked the clock on the wall and cleared his throat. "Night is coming. I've got to get out to the animals. McClendon, please keep us informed."

The chief nodded as Blake and Eli left the house. Then McClendon's face darkened and he straightened up and folded his arms over his chest. He lowered his voice. "Miss Miller, how well do you know Dr. Jamison?"

Abby swallowed hard and sank down into the plush cushions. "I don't. I don't know him at all. I just woke up in the E.R. yesterday and there he was. But since then, he's been very kind—even helping me tidy up my clinic. Why? Should I be concerned?"

McClendon looked toward the back of the house where the others had gone as if to ensure he had privacy to speak. "On a professional level? No. He's got an impeccable record as a doctor, a student. He's been to all the best schools, has worked in top hospitals—on paper, he's...he's flawless. On a personal level I guess that makes me a little nervous. I've known you and your brother for a long time. I just... well, I thought maybe I saw something there between the two of you. I just want you to be cautious."

Something between the two of them? Abby could feel her face heating up like wildfire. Was it that obvious that she was a little bit attracted to him? Goodness. She was going to have to put on a better game face. She swallowed hard and willed away her blushing cheeks. "You think he brought this mess down here to Willow Trace, don't you?"

"I do. But...I also believe him when he says he doesn't know what's going on. Though I've been wrong before so... Anyway, I'm going to be checking all his connections, both personal and professional, on a deeper level. I'll let you know if I see any red flags. Just be more careful. Okay? No more driving alone."

"Of course. You're right."

"Good night, Miss Miller." He headed for the door. "Get some rest and know that I'll have a patrol car circling by."

"Eli won't like that. He still thinks he's a detective."

"Take care of yourself, Miss Miller. I'll check on you in the morning." He left through the front door. Abby heard the sound of his truck starting up and driving away.

With all the men out of the house and Hannah still in the kitchen, Abby slid down into the couch, closing her eyes. Her head ached terribly. Sleepiness must have fogged her thoughts because as she reviewed her conversation with McClendon, it was as if he'd been telling her not to get personally involved with Blake. She'd already decided that herself, and yet the chief's mention of doing more searches struck a chord. She really didn't know much about Blake at all. What harm would it do for her to run a few searches herself?

Abby thought about her laptop. It was sitting there a few feet away, waiting for her to look up Dr. Blake Jamison.

And while she was at it, she might look up a few other things, too.

TEN

Another twenty-minute nap and a good dose of her own healing tea and Abby felt like a new woman. She managed to get herself up from the couch, go upstairs and change out of her bloody clothing, then sit back down with her laptop. Her heart beat hard and steady as she connected to the internet with her AirCard and opened up the browser, unsure how much time she might have before the men returned or before Hannah guilted her into putting the computer away.

First, she typed in *Blake Jamison, Doctor, New York City*. Pages of links popped up—his practice, his doctors' associations, awards, special programs, the foundation and charities he'd mentioned, then articles and articles and articles about Blake, his parents and more. Abby couldn't believe it. Blake was a New York socialite. Like royalty, his whole life was online—photographed and documented by glossy, high-end, who's-who magazines. Abby didn't know where to start reading.

As quickly as she could, Abby skimmed articles about Blake's parents, their charities and huge fancy events. She knew his family was wealthy, but not to this extent.

Blake was the CEO and director of many of these organizations. Some of the articles spoke of his travels around the world to help the needy. On and on, Abby grew dizzy trying to take it all in. No wonder so many people were calling him. He was a big deal. And now she knew why McClendon, like her father, had warned her to be cautious.

She also knew that despite what she'd been telling herself, she did like the doctor. She liked him a lot.

Because if she didn't, seeing this whole other life of his wouldn't have made her feel so hopeless.

After all the charity-event links, Abby saw a page of Google images of Blake. Wow. There was one of him on a yacht. Another showed him shushing down ski slopes. Helping needy children in third-world countries. At a ribbon-cutting ceremony for the opening of a new clinic for the underprivileged. Although this discovery made her aware of the great differences in their social standing, seeing Blake at work and play and knowing how modest he'd been about it all only made him more attractive. Go figure. Abby sighed.

Her cursor stopped over an image of him in a gorgeous tux. In the photo, he was stepping out of a stretch limousine with a beautiful brunette wrapped around his arm—the same lovely woman who had called him at lunch. The caption read "Uptown power couple Blake Jamison and Natalie Jenkins. Sources say he has already been to Tiffany's and is just waiting for the perfect setting to pop the big question."

What? Blake was engaged? He might have mentioned that. No wonder he took the call in the other room. Abby quickly sloughed away her sappy sentiments when looking at the other articles. She had no right to think such things about another woman's fiancé. Now she only wondered what else Blake Jamison was hiding.

With a grunt, she aimed her finger down at the mouse, ready to close the search.

But she didn't. There was something that kept catching her eye. And somehow it seemed as if it might be important. Almost every single image of Blake had the same owner imprint across it—Daveux.

She wasn't sure if that meant Daveux owned the photo or took the photo or what. Sheltered in her Willow Trace upbringing, Abby knew next to nothing about the photo-journalism business. But the consistency there sparked her interest. She enlarged one of the pictures so that she could read the whole name glossed over the image. Phillipe Daveux.

There was a link to his website. She clicked it.

Lots and lots of celebrity shots. Pages of fabulous, dazzling photos. Abby recognized some of the faces. Others were unfamiliar to her. Blake had his very own section of images by Daveux. Obviously, this photographer knew a lot about Blake and his family. Under many of the photos were links to articles that Daveux had written. Most of the articles had been published in a magazine called *New York Ways.*

Abby shrugged. She'd never heard of that, either. Blake lived in a whole other world from her—a world where people followed him around and took pictures of him and wrote articles; a world where he owned over ten different businesses and was responsible for other people's jobs; a world where he was engaged to a beautiful woman named Natalie; a world where Abby would never belong....

Blake matched Eli's long strides across the rolling pasture leading to the barn. The bleating flock of sheep looked nearly invisible against the hillside, blanketed in snow. Some of the small, fluffy animals skittered toward the barn as they approached.

"No one was expecting this weather," Eli said, "including the animals. They look ready to get inside and get warm and dry."

"So, what's the procedure?"

"Well, if you will just slide open the barn doors and stand in the aisle at the second gate, I'll herd them in. With you blocking the back of the aisle, they'll file into the first holding pen. Make sure that gate is open. It should be."

"I think I can do that." Blake headed to the great-barn door. He slid it to the left and walked inside the large structure. The air was warm and surprisingly dry. The second gate was open, so Blake positioned himself just a step farther down the long aisle. Seconds later, he heard a rumbling of hooves. He turned just in time to watch the first of the little critters race into the dry, straw-filled pen. Eli brought up the end of the line, giving one or two of the more reluctant ones a little push on the rear.

"Lock the gate," Eli instructed after he chased them into the pen.

Blake shut and pinned the gate. Eli smiled as he hopped effortlessly over the high railing and touched Blake's shoulder. "Cows next."

Following Eli's lead, Blake helped repeat a similar but slightly more challenging process with the small herd of cattle. Soon the barn was filled with the animals' warmth and smells and sounds. Blake found himself smiling at the sight—it looked like a Norman Rockwell Christmas card, only it was the month of April.

"Wow. That was kind of fun." Blake laughed, then paused to take an awkwardly long step over a pile of manure. "I guess you can tell I haven't been around many farm animals."

"We'll make a farmer of you yet." Eli patted him on the back.

They stepped outside, and Blake took in a long, deep breath of the fresh, snow-filled air. "I have to admit that it's extremely pleasant here. I like it much more than I'd anticipated."

Eli nodded. "I missed this place—the smells, the sounds, the people—every day when I lived in Philadelphia. Don't get me wrong, I'm glad I was a cop for ten years. But now I'm so glad I'm home."

The word *home* stung Blake's ears. "Home. I feel like I don't have one right now. I suppose that's why I'm here. Without my parents, New York suddenly didn't feel like home anymore."

Eli's expression grew dim. "After dinner last night, Abigail told us about your loss. I'm very sorry. My *dat* and I have our issues—as you saw this morning—but I can't imagine losing him. Nor my *mamm*." He looked back dreamily toward the house. "Nor Hannah."

Blake swallowed hard. Eli's words tightened the band of ever-present loneliness that strangled his heart. "Thank you. It was difficult to make the decision to leave so much in limbo back home to be here. But in the end, it felt like the right thing to do. I only wish it were going a little smoother."

"You are having difficulties with your search? I didn't know that," Eli said. "As I said last night, I will be happy to help you in any way I can. I did used to be a detective."

Blake smiled at Eli's humor. He wondered how one sibling could be so intense and the other so seemingly laidback. "Actually, it looks like the lawyer I was hoping to get information through is unavailable. I'll have to call back the man in New York who helped me with the contact here and see if he knows anything. But I suppose my next move would be to comb through public birth records. Not sure how that works…and I'm surprised you want to help. Your sister doesn't really approve of my plan to find my birth parents."

"I think my sister likes to claim opinions on many subjects that she has little experience with." Eli lifted his eyebrows playfully.

"What else should I know about your sister?" Blake laughed.

"Too much to tell you between here and the house." Eli laughed with him. "But in all seriousness, I can hook you up with the Lancaster Public Records. If you know specifically which township, that would save you a lot of time."

"According to the file my mother passed on to me, the transaction was signed in Millersville. The document doesn't reveal the names of my birth parents, but it does state that Willow Trace was their town of residence," Blake shared in a tentative voice.

"Okay, then. The old Hall of Records. I'll take you there on Monday."

"That would be great."

"If you don't mind, I might look into this lawyer that you went to see. If an office was there and then moved, all within one day, someone had to see it happen. Let's look into that." Eli stopped alongside the whitewashed four-board fence. He stretched his arms over the top rail and leaned back. Looking out over his land, his expression was a mixture of deep thought and curiosity. "Too many strange things are happening. We need to figure out how this is all connected."

Blake stood against the wooden fence next to Eli, watching the heavy snow tumble through the air. So many thoughts scrambled through his head. "I've been wondering, too, if..."

A dark figure flashed between trees in the distance. Blake turned to Eli. "Did you see that?"

Eli followed the direction of Blake's gaze across the rolling pastures and into the distance. It wasn't difficult to detect the dark movement against the sea of white snow that lay before them.

"I did." Abby's brother sprang into motion. "Come on. I think we can catch him. It might just be one of the teen boys who live nearby, but no one should be passing through here this time of night. Especially in this weather."

Blake fell in behind Eli as they tromped through the snow over the adjacent pasture and toward the dark figure. Their target moved away, but not nearly at the pace Eli could maintain. Blake struggled to keep up with Abby's brother as they climbed a steep hill. But a better view of the dark figure made him forget the burning lactic acid in his thighs. The dark figure was certainly dressed as an Amish man—short, dark wool coat, black trousers and black brimmed hat—but he was no teenager. He was a man, and judging by the white hair peeking out from under the brim of his black hat, an older man.

"Do you recognize him?" Blake asked.

"No," Eli said over his shoulder. "But he's no teenager. I don't know who he is."

That it was a stranger seemed to alarm Eli even more for he somehow increased his already frantic pace. The man picked up his own pace, running toward the nearby woods.

Blake and Eli reached the edge of the woods where the man had disappeared. The forest was thick but Blake could just make out the lumber mill situated on the other side. The two men forged their way through the woods, following the set of fresh footprints that cut between the scattered birch trees toward the mill. The old wooden structure loomed as a daunting figure against the late-evening sky.

Blake and Eli came to a screeching halt at the edge of the woods as a large black sedan blazed around the corner of the building. It raced along the side of the mill—heading straight for them.

The two men scrambled back into the cover of the trees as the vehicle swung at them, just missing the closest trunk. Blake noted that the grill of the car was badly dinged and the passenger side was scratched and dented. The car flew past them, screeching its wheels as it slowed to take a left out onto the highway that ran in front of the mill.

Blake ran after the car to the edge of the road, watching as it disappeared behind the next hill. "I think that was the car that hit Abby. Did you see the dents along the side?"

"Yeah. I did." Eli stopped beside him. "But I didn't get the license-plate numbers. The car was moving so fast. Did you see anything?"

"No. But I'm thinking it must have been the man in the woods that we were following."

"I'm sure it was, even though he was dressed Amish."

"I think first we should go back and check on the ladies. We've been gone for a long time. I'm starting to think that we should never have left."

ELEVEN

"You must be feeling better." The strain in Blake's face had lessened considerably since he and her brother had entered the house. They'd explained about the strange man in Amish clothing and the black car at the mill. Hannah and Eli had gone into the kitchen to put dinner on the table, insisting that Abby stay in the sitting room and entertain their guest.

Abby suspected that her brother had taken quite a liking to Blake and was aiming to get them to know each other better by leaving them alone. If he'd seen the pictures of Blake in a tux with a beautiful brunette on his arm and knew what Abby did about his money and fiancée and celebrity status, she was pretty sure he would change his mind about getting all chummy.

"Yes, much better." She had resumed her seat on the couch that she'd occupied most of the evening. Blake sat across from her in the most uncomfortable but closest chair to her spot. His nearness made her a bit uneasy. Or maybe it was the way he fiddled with the wool hat Eli hat lent him. He'd made a job of staring at it and twirling it between his fingers. He only lacked a pair of black trousers and suspenders and he would have passed for a member of the *Ordnung*.

"I can't believe the guy that ran you off the road was right there," Blake said, startling her out of her thoughts. "So close. And we couldn't do anything to stop him."

"Was he tall and heavyset with cold, gray eyes?"

Blake looked up with a start. "No, in fact, he was quite the opposite. Well, we weren't close enough to see his eyes, but he had a slight frame. He was fast. And so is your brother."

Abby smiled. "Eli may not have caught him this time, but he won't give up. Persistence is one of my brother's greatest flaws—and virtues." Thinking back over what she'd learned earlier that evening, she realized that that quality could also be used to describe the photojournalist who so diligently captured every event in Blake's life. "Hey...does the name Daveux mean anything to you?" *How about Natalie?*

Blake scratched his head and looked pensive. But before he offered an answer, Abby's cell phone chimed. She pulled the phone from her pocket and read the screen. "It's one of the prepaid numbers. Must be a patient."

He nodded.

"Hello?"

"Abigail. *Doomla*—hurry." The Pennsylvania Dutch sounded a bit anxious. "It's time. Anna is going to have her baby tonight."

"*Ja,* Mr. Brenneman, rest easy. How far apart are the contractions?"

"Two minutes."

Two minutes? That meant the baby was coming very soon. With all the snow, would they even make it? She had to try. Abby stood and headed for the stairs so she could grab her things from the upstairs bedroom. "I'll be there as soon as I can," she promised before hanging up the phone.

"What? Where are you going?" Blake asked. "You're not in any shape to go anywhere."

"I forgot. I don't even have a car." Abby stopped at the edge of the stairs, completely ignoring Blake's comment. "I guess I can take Eli's horse and buggy. That will take forever, though."

"Are you not listening to me?" Blake stood and headed toward her. "You can't go anywhere. You've been in a serious accident."

"I have a patient with a baby to deliver." She started up the stairs. She would need her coat and her car keys to open the trunk.

"I'll go. I can deliver a baby. Or they can go to the hospital." He grabbed her elbow before she passed the third step. "You have to stay here."

Abby swung around, not realizing how close he stood behind her. Their faces were inches apart. She looked away and brushed her hair off her shoulder. "I appreciate your concern, but I have to go and you can't do anything to stop me."

"Time for dinner." Eli entered the room, eyeing them curiously. "What's the matter?"

Abby explained the situation. "Anna shouldn't deliver for another week or so. I have to be there."

"They should call an ambulance," Blake said. "Or I could go."

"Not going to happen." Abby couldn't keep the frustration from her voice. Blake was wasting time arguing with her.

"Abby is right, Blake," Eli said quickly. "The Brennemans will not be comfortable with anyone but her. They won't call an ambulance, either. But you should take her. Go together. It's not far. You should be fine in Blake's car.

If not, you can ride a horse or get as close as you can and walk the rest of the way."

Abby froze on the step as her brother told them what to do and how to do it. He was turning into the proverbial Amish head of the family. The only thing lacking was a houseful of children, and judging by the new snugness in the waistline of Hannah's frock, it wouldn't be long before the first one joined their home.

Abby was just grateful that this time, the patriarch was on her side. She smiled and turned to Blake. "He's right. I have to go. But if you would drive I would be very grateful."

"Yes, this plan I can live with." He grabbed his coat from the back of the chair and waited for her at the front door.

In less than three minutes, the two of them were out the door, in Blake's car and halfway down the snowy drive.

"Stop at the ditch with my car. I have to get my medical kit."

Blake drove carefully through the snow, which, thankfully, had all but stopped falling. Blake threw the car into Park just across from her Malibu. "I'll get it. In the trunk?"

"Yes. Thank you." Abby handed him the keys, then watched him cross the street, grab her equipment and return. He climbed back in behind the wheel and passed her things to her.

"Thanks. And thanks for taking me. It's not far to the Brennemans'. Just turn left here and go about a mile down the main street. It's within a little cluster of homes on the right."

"It's my pleasure." Blake drove on, turning onto the main road. "You know, that name you mentioned just before the phone call seemed really familiar but I can't quite put my finger on it. What was it again? Devero? Is that someone at the hospital?"

Abby swallowed hard at the reminder of the distance between them. "Daveux. He's a celebrity photojournalist in New York. You didn't tell me you were a celebrity."

"What? I'm not." Blake frowned, with an air of confusion about his face.

"I looked you up on Google. You are. And so were your parents. I read about all the good things all of you have done."

"That doesn't make me a celebrity."

"A photojournalist has a whole page of his website devoted to you. That sounds like celebrity status to me."

"Well, it's not." Blake shook his head. "Listen, Abby. I'm a doctor. Not a celebrity. And yes, my parents gave a lot of money away and they liked all of that attention. But I don't. So there—there's another reason I left New York. And so what? What's this all got to do with anything?"

"I don't feel like you've been honest with me about who you are. You're a socialite. Isn't that what you call it?"

"My parents were socialites. Not me. You say things with such certainty, but you are not right about everything. And you really aren't right about me. Sometimes I think you repeat your conviction about becoming a nurse because really deep down inside you wonder if you should have given it up and done what your father wanted. You're no different than I am. Neither of us can figure out what's ahead."

Abby could hardly take Blake's painfully true words. Not even her own brother had dared to say those things to her. She swallowed hard and sucked in a difficult breath.

"And why were you investigating me on Google?"

"I felt like I wanted to…" She could feel his disapproving gaze on her. Ugh. Why did she even care? Why was she listening to a word he said? Wasn't he engaged? Perhaps she should mention that she saw his fiancée in the pictures. *Probably not.* Abby shook her head. She was being ridiculous. She had to get all these silly, petty thoughts out of her head and concentrate on what was important. "I don't know. I thought I might find something that would help us figure out why people are trying to kill us."

He dropped his head.

"Turn right here." She pointed to the small, gray stone cottage to the right. He had her so flustered with all of this talk that she'd almost missed the turnoff. "So, have you ever even delivered a baby?"

"I had a rotation through Obstetrics." Blake managed a weak smile as he parked the car. "Does that mean I get to assist?"

"If Anna and Benjamin are comfortable with you," she said, turning toward him as she opened the car door. "I don't see why not."

Blake's eyes met hers. He reached over and took hold of her hand. He leaned close to her and her pulse doubled in speed.

"Abigail, I am who I say I am. I haven't hidden anything from you. I'm nothing more than a doctor from New York who just found out he was adopted. That's it. I'm certainly nothing special. And if this mess we've gotten into has anything to do with me or my parents or any part of my life in New York, I promise you I don't know how or why. You have to believe me."

Abby held her breath. His hand on hers and his pleading brown eyes had her feeling so uncertain. After a long moment, she managed to nod. "Let's get inside."

Despite Abby's expectations, the labor was not fast. A long evening stretched into an even longer night and Abby couldn't have been more thankful for Blake's presence. Her head and body needed too much rest for her to have handled the delivery alone. The Brennemans were charmed by Blake's humble and helpful demeanor. The baby came slowly, but he was healthy—small, but strong and able to breathe. For that, Abby stopped and thanked God.

By morning, a screaming Gideon Brenneman was ruling the roost while Anna was resting in her room. The sun was out and melting the unexpected snow more quickly than it had fallen. By 8:00 a.m., she and Blake said their goodbyes and were about to head back to her brother's.

"I don't think I've ever enjoyed being a doctor more than I did in these past few hours." Blake opened his car door for her. "Thank you."

His soft brown eyes caught her again. *A woman could get lost in those eyes.* But she wouldn't. There was nothing for her there. They were from different worlds. She'd known it before, but seeing those pictures of him on the internet had really driven the reality of that home. The beautiful, sophisticated woman who had called Blake just the day before—*that* was the type of woman who needed to be with a man like Blake. They lived in a world she did not belong to and never would.

"I'm glad you were there. I couldn't have handled it alone. I'm exhausted."

"You must be." He closed her door and drove her to her brother's. "Get some rest. I'll see you Monday."

Abby was glad he wasn't coming inside. "What's Monday?"

"Eli is taking me to the Hall of Records so that I can go through the birth records."

What? Why was her brother getting so involved in Blake's personal business? Especially concerning this adoption. Abby held in her shocked reaction. She thanked Blake again, then scrambled up the front porch and went straight to the guest room. She would confront Eli later, after a few hours of rest.

Abby lay down, closed her eyes and fell into a fitful sleep.

"I can't thank you enough for letting me look through these files, Mrs. Betts." Blake tucked the folder of documents under his left arm and surveyed the crowded filing room. It was stuffed with floor-to-ceiling cabinets with drawers and drawers of birth records.

A sole computer station had been set up in the far corner.

"Of course, we had all the records converted to electronic files years ago. They can be accessed from any government computers if you know the right codes. This station will give you direct access to Lancaster County."

Blake laughed. "It's just like the hospitals. Everything is electronic, but no one throws away the paperwork, just in case."

"I'm going out for lunch. If you find what you need, you can print or make copies over there." She pointed to a large Xerox machine next to the computer station. "Please lock the front door if you leave before I get back."

"Are you sure? I can come back later if this is inconvenient." Blake made the offer more out of politeness than sincerity. He had little time before he was needed back at the hospital. Dr. Dodd, the head administrator at Fairview, had been less than happy that he'd taken off the past couple of days, regardless of it being a firm request directly from the chief of police.

"I'm completely sure. This is all public record and if Eli trusts you, then so do I."

"Thank you."

Mrs. Betts left the small documents room, closing a

thick metal door behind her. The air felt instantly still, as if the administrative assistant had sucked all of it away with her. The old documents gave the room a dank, unpleasant odor. Hopefully, his search would be fast. Blake was not much for tight, closed-in spaces with no windows.

He sat down at the one computer station, placing his own file folder—the one with the letter from his mother—on the small desk. He waved the mouse, and the screen lit up with a typical search page. He typed in his birth year, month and day, and hit Enter.

A swirling circle popped up. *Loading. Loading. Loading.* He sat back in the old office chair. What did he hope to accomplish through this search? Maybe a doctor's name. He wasn't sure. It was quite possible that his Amish birth parents didn't even use a doctor for the delivery. He doubted that thirty years ago many of them did. He'd learned a few nights ago from Abby that not too many now did, either.

The wheel continued to swirl around the screen. *Abby.* She'd been on Blake's mind ever since he'd dropped her at her brother's after the all-night delivery—a night that he would never forget. It was the first time in a long time that his work, his medicine, felt good—felt as if it made a difference.

It was the way he'd wanted his work to be—the way his mom and dad had always talked about their mission trips. And being there with Abigail, watching her work, had made it even more special. At least to him, it had felt special. He wasn't so sure she'd thought so. Then again, she'd been so tired she'd hardly been able to talk. And she was so mad at him about the internet articles and all that other nonsense in his life back home. He had to admit he didn't miss it, any of it, not one bit.

He'd hoped to see her today. He'd thought she'd still be

with Eli that morning, but she wasn't. Her friend Janice from the hospital had picked her up and taken her to get a rental car while hers was in the shop. As soon as he finished at the Hall of Records he planned to call her.

The screen had gone dark. He wiggled the mouse. The screen relit.

No data for date provided.

Of course. He threw his hands in the air. That would have been too easy.

Think. Think. Think.

Blake returned to the search screen. He typed in the same information for year and month but left the day blank. This time the swirling wheel lasted only a few seconds before turning up three-hundred-plus entries.

Blake's heart leaped as he scrolled down the list of surnames. Jamison, of course, was not going to be there. However, it wasn't too difficult to spot some of the Amish surnames. But still there were so many. He needed to refine his search.

Male births.

The three hundred entries dropped to less than one hundred and twenty. Now he might thin these out by location.

Willow Trace.

He was down to twenty. Blake smiled. That number he could manage. Blake began to read through each file, paying particular attention to the ones with Amish surnames. Most of those listed Dr. Miles as the doctor. There were none from the day that he'd always known as his birthday, so Blake double-checked the four records that were nearest that date. All of those listed Dr. Miles. He printed those records. He was pretty certain that Eli or even Abigail might be able to tell him if they knew these families. Maybe it would lead to something. Maybe it wouldn't. Talking to this Dr. Miles might be worth a try, as well.

Blake collected his things and stood from the computer station when he heard footsteps passing in the hallway outside the door. Mrs. Betts must have returned from lunch, although that seemed a bit quick, he thought as he checked his watch.

"Mrs. Betts?"

There was no answer. She probably couldn't hear him through that thick door. Oh, well. He'd see her on the way out, which was exactly where he was headed.

But as he passed through the maze of filing cabinets, he happened to see that he was standing right by the files containing his own birth year. He paused. Why not take a peek?

He rolled open the drawer and pulled out the thick file for November of that year, his birth month. Just eyeballing it, his guess was the file had a lot more than three hundred records. Suddenly, he forgot all about leaving. *What if some of the records didn't make it into the computer?* Blake shook his head. The files would have been entered from microfiche years ago, read by an electronic laser or something of that sort to get everything computerized.... How could they have missed anything?

Still, out of curiosity, he sat back at the desk, opened the folder and began to turn through the records. The task proved more interesting than he'd imagined. On the computer, there had been no births in Willow Trace on his birthdate. But in this folder, there were three. All male. All delivered by Dr. Miles. One listed John and Jane Doe as birth parents.

Blake grabbed the file with a shaking hand. He made a quick copy, replaced the folder and headed to the door. As soon as he could, he would find this Dr. Miles and hope he could lead him to the truth. It was something. And it gave him hope.

Blake turned the large metal handle of the thick door. He was more than ready to get out of that tiny closet of a room. But the handle wouldn't budge. Blake shook the handle and tried again.

"Mrs. Betts?" Had she locked him inside accidentally? If Blake hadn't felt claustrophobic before, he sure did now. "Mrs. Betts?"

He shook the door again.

Nothing.

He put his file folder to the side and studied the door handle. Oddly, it looked as though it locked from the inside. Blake turned the button lock one way and then the other but it was no use.

He was locked inside.

Blake pulled his cell phone from his pocket. Except it wasn't in his pocket. He'd left it inside the car.

Of course…his new habit inspired by Hannah Miller.

Blake made his way back through the maze of file folders to the computer station. He hoped there was a phone there.

TWELVE

Abby spent her morning rushing from here to there in the rental car she'd picked up, stopping at the hospital, her home, the body shop and at the police station for a quick conversation with Chief McClendon. According to him, a Detective Day of the FBI had taken over the investigation of Hancock's murder and would be in touch with her if necessary. At this point all he knew was that they were focusing on identifying Hancock and trying to make connections in New York City. McClendon warned her that both she and Dr. Jamison might have FBI tails. He'd also asked her to pass on the information to Dr. Jamison, which she had reluctantly agreed to do.

Truth was she wanted to avoid Blake as much as possible. She didn't like the way she felt around him. He was too rich and cool and confident. She was plain and awkward and unsophisticated. She didn't like how he'd just come to town to serve his own curiosity about his birth parents. What if he created a wake of heartache behind him? Had he even thought about that?

There was more, too. She didn't like the way he looked at her with those chocolate-brown eyes—the way he had that whole night when he'd helped with the delivery. Of course, she couldn't help but admire his skills as a doctor. He'd been amazing. Hard to believe he was the same man in all those internet pictures. How could he be? Abby shook her head. She didn't know and it didn't matter. Blake was all wrong for her and all wrong *about* her. She knew exactly what she wanted and it had nothing to do with him. She just had to deliver this message and then she could leave Blake to his own affairs.

Abby pulled up in front of the Hall of Records. Blake's Land Rover was parked in front. She knew Eli had arranged for him to have access to the Lancaster birth records.

A wave of unease fell over Abby as she parked next to Blake's car. The building looked abandoned. There were no other cars in front. This was a small operation, a satellite office to the main town hall, run by a skeleton staff.

This won't take but a second, she thought, leaving her handbag in the car. She pushed open the double doors leading inside.

"Yoo-hoo," she called out.

The front desk sat empty. It was dead quiet. Abby turned her head, peering around the room. Nothing much in the small room but a few chairs and a reception desk. Behind the desk was a hallway leading to the other offices. She glanced back through the glass window of the front doors, feeling more and more uneasy. The parking lot was still empty but at least across the street was a mini-mart, which had a few customers. Seeing busy people nearby should have reassured her a bit, but it didn't.

Oh, Abby, you're being silly. Just find Blake and get this over and done.

Abby followed the narrow hallway toward the center of the building. "Blake?"

"Abigail?" his voice answered back from the far end of the hall.

"Yes, it's Abby." She looked around. "Where are you?"

"I'm in here. Locked in here. I can't get this door open." A big metal door at the end of the hallway shook. "I wanted to call you, but I left my cell phone in the car."

Abby smiled. No wonder he sounded panicked. He'd locked himself in the filing room. "Hold on. I'll be right there."

She tried the doorknob. *Click.* It opened easily.

"Wow." Blake came out of the room, looking flushed and out of breath. "I do not like being enclosed in small spaces. Thank you. That was so creepy. How long have you been in the building?"

"Not even a minute. Why?"

"I don't know." He shrugged. "I thought I heard someone walking down the hallway a few minutes ago."

"It wasn't me." Abby shivered. "Actually, there isn't another car in the parking lot. No one around. I was feeling pretty creepy coming in this empty old building. Where's the receptionist?"

"She went to lunch."

"And just left you alone here?"

"She said she trusted any friend of Eli's." He tugged at her arm and pulled her inside the filing room. His coloring was normal again and he looked almost giddy with excitement. "Come here. Look."

"Blake? You really want to go back into that room?" she teased.

"Good point." He propped the door open with a wedge. "Now it's safe. I want to show you what I found."

"Your parents?" She followed him into the stuffy room to where he stopped at a table that held an open file folder.

"No. Adoption records are sealed for the most part. I

didn't really expect to find that. But I didn't expect to find this, either."

Blake spread out several file copies that he'd made. Each of them was a birth close to the same date. Abby recognized a few of the family names—Amish names. Blake pointed to the line that indicated the attending physician. "Look. All of these families used the same doctor."

"Dr. Nathan Miles," Abby read with a frown. "I've never heard of him."

"Well, this was thirty years ago—he could have retired or passed away by now." Blake pulled out the last photocopy and showed it to Abby. "But I think he may have delivered me—I mean this could be me. Same birthdate. Same doctor. Jane and John Doe parents."

"Amazing. Now you can look for this doctor. Right?" She forced a smile for him even though she still had a bad feeling about his search.

"Yes. I could even talk to these other families who were having babies at the same time with the same doctor, too. They might remember who else was expecting at the same time."

Abby shook her head.

"What? You don't like that idea, either?"

"You can try, Blake. But Amish families are not going to talk to you as freely as you might think."

He smiled and touched his hand to her chin, looking as if he'd conquered the world. "That's why you're going to go with me and help."

She locked eyes with him—his chocolate eyes that sucked her in and made her forget about everything else in the world. Did he feel that when he looked at her? He had to feel something—she could see it in his face as he leaned toward her, his gaze on her mouth.

"I've never met anyone like you, Abby. You—"

Whooph.

Abby and Blake pulled apart as a flash of light glowed at them from the hallway.

"What was that?" Blake tossed the file papers down and raced toward the hallway.

Abby followed but stopped short behind him as she felt the heat coming from the corridor.

"The only exit is on fire." Blake turned to her. "There's no way out."

Abby tried to lunge past him.

"Stay back, Abby. There's some sort of accelerator on that. It's spreading fast." He pulled her back behind him into the filing room.

Flames lined the hallway to the front office. They flew higher and hotter, inching closer to the end of the hallway and the room they were now trapped in.

"Please tell me there's a phone in here." Abby looked at him anxiously.

"I'm not sure. I was going to check earlier, but then you showed up." Blake headed back to the computer station. "If there is one, I think it would be back here."

"Or we could use the computer to contact someone," Abby suggested, following him back.

Blake located the small office phone plugged in behind the computer. He lifted the receiver to his ear. "It's dead."

Abby was already beside him trying the computer. "No internet. It's probably all connected."

"Someone has trapped us in here for good." Blake looked around at the walls and the ceiling. "Should we close the metal door? Maybe it's fireproof."

Blake crossed the room.

Abby was right beside him. She stopped him from closing the door. "If you shut that then we are definitely locked in here."

He looked down the hallway at the hungry flames, already halfway to the filing room, devouring the old dry wood. "We're already locked in."

Blake scratched his head. What could they do? They had to do something. If they didn't, they'd be sitting ducks.

Just as someone had planned for them to be.

Blake looked around the room again—and then he looked up. The drop ceiling was low and tiled. The rooms might be connected through the ceiling ductwork. If the fire was contained to the hallway, perhaps they could maneuver around it and make their way to the front of the building.

"I've got an idea." Blake hopped up on top of the closest filing cabinet. Being a good six foot two, he merely needed to rest on his knees on the top of the metal structure and he had access to the tiles above.

"Good thinking." Abby was already hopping up onto the adjacent filing cabinet.

Together they lifted away the closest overhead tile and peered up through the space. The air was hotter there but not yet as smoky—the flames from the hallway had just begun to reach the height of the ceiling.

"I can crawl across that beam." Abby started to lift herself into the ceiling structure.

"Maybe not." He grabbed her arm just as the framework began to bend under her weight. "Those flames are going to eat through the ceiling tiles like termites on wood. But at least we can see that the front of the building is clear. We could get out if we could just find a way to get there."

Abby pointed down. "How about that?"

Blake followed her gaze to the lower side wall. There

was a small space between two filing cabinets and behind it was an air return.

Blake nodded. They both hopped down to the floor and inspected the screen.

"We need a screwdriver," Abby said.

Blake took an ink pen from his pocket and ripped the clip from the front of it. Holding only the small, flat part of the clip, he maneuvered it into the screwhead. It took both hands to hold it in place but slowly he was able to loosen the bolts and remove the return cover.

"Look. It goes down under the building." Blake pointed behind the grate. Just the sight of the downward duct-work caused hope to return to his smoke-filled head. He grabbed Abby's shoulders and kissed her out of sheer joy. "We can get out."

Abby smiled, though she looked a little puzzled by his quick peck on the lips. She might have been blushing, but then again, the red in her face could have been from the ever-building heat that encircled them. Closer and closer.

Blake reached into the return with both arms and yanked the ductwork away from the wall. Just as he had hoped, the large metal cylinder-shaped tubing dropped away and cold, musty air flowed over them from under the building.

"You first." He smiled at Abby, who looked as relieved as he felt. She slid over to the gigantic hole in the wall that he'd created.

"Crawl to a vent and push your way out. I'll be right behind you."

Blake grabbed hold of Abby's arms and was helping her to get her legs down under the building when she squirmed one hand loose from him. "Your files. Go grab your files."

Blake smiled. He stood and reached over to the desk

area where he'd spread out his findings to show Abby before the fire had started. He scooped them up, tucked them under his arm and slid down under the building after Abby.

THIRTEEN

Abby's arms and hands clutched deeply into the cold, wet, gravelly muck under the old Hall of Records auxiliary building. It was wonderful to breathe in the damp, smoke-free air, but her lungs were still full of fumes, and she coughed continually as she groped along the floor.

Where to go?

Abby turned around on all fours. The hallway's flames had eaten through that area of the building. From the underside, it looked like a great bluish-orange ball of lava churning in midair. The fire was spreading out to all four sides of the building. They would have to stick to the edge of the stone foundation to make their way out...if there *was* a way out.

Blake dropped down beside her. In the orange glow, she could see his sooty cheeks and his dirt-coated hands. He had to crouch even lower than she did to fit under the flooring. But he seemed to have his bearings as he touched her elbow and motioned to the back wall. He scurried along first and she followed. It was slow moving as the dirt floor seemed to rise up, leaving less and less space for their bodies.

"We're almost there. I see the vent. It's just ahead." Blake looked back at her. Probably heard her gasping and coughing even through the rumbling roar of the flames. "You okay?"

Abby was nodding when the unmistakable sound of splitting wood cracked overhead. Abby scooted back instinctively, while Blake moved forward. There was a terrible ripping sound as the beam just over them began to split.

"Get back!" Blake yelled.

Abby was already scrambling as quickly as she could on her hands and knees until she hit the edge of the stone foundation. As quickly as the beam split, flames licked around it from the center outward, racing from the start of the wood all the way to the end, which had fallen between them, leaving her and Blake divided by a wall of fire. And the only way out was on his side of the beam.

Abby fought her tears—they would do her no good here.

It was no use. Blake could not get around the fallen burning beam, which separated him from Abigail. He couldn't even see her or hear her, but he knew that she had been forced into the far back-left corner of the building's foundation. It was shallow there and with fire blocking her, there would not be much oxygen for long.

This was all his fault. His stupid quest to find his birth parents. If he hadn't been at the Hall of Records looking up birth records, they wouldn't have gotten caught in this fire.

Or was this just a continuation of the attacks by the man from the hospital, still after Abigail? It was hard to know. It was all starting to blur together for Blake. And anyway, what difference did it make? Right now what mattered was saving Abigail. If only he knew how.

Blake turned reluctantly away from the fallen beam and Abigail and slid the next few feet to the panel of the foundation vent.

"Please do not be locked," he prayed aloud.

Blake pressed on the wood panel, and much to his relief, it punched out of the cut frame with great ease.

The opening wasn't large but it was large enough. Blake began to squeeze through the small hole. Sunlight. Fresh air. Cold, fresh air. And voices.

"Here he is!"

In seconds, two firefighters had him under the arms and cleared him from the foundation of the old building. As soon as Blake was on his feet, someone draped a huge blanket around him. Slowly, his vision readjusted from being inside the dark crawl space.

With a cough, he grabbed the arm of the closest firefighter. "Abby's in the corner. Blocked. You have to get her out."

One of the two firefighters grabbed a sledgehammer from the truck and went running to the spot Blake had indicated. The far-left corner of the building.

"Are you sure she's here?" he asked. "There's not much clearance."

"A beam fell down the center of the crawl space when we were heading for the vent. It closed her in. She has to be here." *If she hasn't already been burned or asphyxiated...* He couldn't stand to think of what might have happened to her.

"We'll have to cut out the mortar and take the stones out one by one. Otherwise we could do more damage than good," said the other firefighter.

Blake was ready to grab the hammer and have a go at the wall himself. The building was already collapsing. They were wasting precious seconds.

The firefighter with the hammer fixed his stance on the uneven ground and began knocking at the bricks hard enough to crumble some of the mortar. A couple of stones broke loose and fell to the ground.

"We're coming in through the corner," yelled the other worker. "Cover your head."

Blake doubted she could hear them. Even if she could, he doubted there was much she could do to get out of the way. If she was even conscious...

"There can't be much air left in there. Hurry!" Blake yelled.

A second hit of the hammer knocked a small three-inch hole at the edge of the corner. Blake stood back, anxious and panicked, but also amazed at the careful approach of the two workers. With another stone held at an angle, the firefighter was able to hit down at the foundation instead of inward. The stonework crumbled under the next few blows. Once the opening was about a foot wide, the other worker lay prostrate on the grass and reached into the dark space under the building.

Blake fell to his knees when he saw Abigail's arms and hands wrapped around those of the firefighter's as he pulled her from under the building. Covered in soot and dirt, the worker slid her out facedown onto the grass. Blake moved in to help, but the hand of an EMT pulled him back.

"You need medical attention," the EMT said.

Blake shook the man off. "I'm fine. I'm a doctor. I'm fine."

His focus was completely on Abby, scanning her head to toe, looking for any sign of life. *Please be okay. Lord, she has to be okay.*

Finally, he detected the expansion of her lungs. She was breathing.

Thank You, Lord. Thank You.

Following the EMTs as they strapped her to the gurney, he watched her eyes flicker. He wanted to cry for joy. He may have only known Abigail Miller for a few days, but it was long enough to know that the world was a better place with her in it.

Thank You, Lord, he thought again as he aligned himself alongside the EMTs and offered his assistance, much more politely than the manner in which he'd refused theirs.

She had two third-degree burns on her right forearm and was blue in the lips and face from lack of oxygen. Her eyes flickered as he helped attach the oxygen mask. Once that was situated, Blake took a close look at her pupils and the contusions made on the front and back of her head earlier in the week.

A cold compress to her burns caused her to awaken with a start.

She patted his arm with her left hand as he wiped away some of the dirt and debris from her cheeks. She was so beautiful, he thought, even like this, even plain and dirty and beat-up. She was so strong—like his mother.

Her fingers wrapped around his hand and pulled at him. He bent over her. "Just relax, Abby. They're going to take you to the hospital. You need treatment on those burns. I'll go with you."

"I'm so sorry," she whispered. "I'm so sorry."

Blake shook his head. She was sorry? More like he was sorry. This was all his fault—him and his stupid idea to find his birth parents, an idea that he was pretty certain he would let go of after this. In fact, maybe it was time for him to get back to New York. He looked at Abby and those feelings she inspired in him stirred again. Yes, for more reasons than one, he needed to get back to New York.

"I couldn't save all of the documents," she whispered. "I tried, but I couldn't reach them. I'm so sorry. I know how much that meant to you. I'm so sorry, Blake."

With her left hand, Abby slid a square of folded papers from under the corner of her blouse. She had tucked them away for him. More guilt weighed at Blake's conscience. What if McClendon was right and all of this mess that was happening was his fault? He should never have come to Lancaster.

Blake climbed into the ambulance and sat beside Abigail, ready for the ride to the hospital. His left hand kept hold of Abby's and in his right he had the few documents she'd saved for him—the letter from his mother, the anonymous birth record on his birthday and three more birth records from the same year with Jane and John Doe listed as parents, all delivered by the same Dr. Nathan Miles.

Blake took in a deep breath and exhaled slowly, thinking about where he should be and what he should be doing. Why had he come down to Lancaster? More and more, he was thinking that Abby might be right. The search for his birth parents might only cause grief and pain, not to himself but to the very people connected to him. Nothing good was going to come out of his selfish quest. He could see that now—he just wished he'd realized it before he'd hurt Abigail. He swallowed hard as he looked at her burns and watched her drag in each breath of air. Blake had some serious thinking to do.

He turned his head and glanced out the back windows as the ambulance slowly pulled away from the burning building. The fire was getting under control but it had already done its damage. The roof was gone and the entire center frame of the old structure was now cinders. Only some of the brick-and-stone outer structure remained—it was a pretty safe assumption that no documents were left in that document room.

In the distance, Blake saw a group of Amish and *Englisch* onlookers watching the firefighters at work.

And while he couldn't be 100 percent sure, it looked to Blake as if off to the side of that group stood the same Amish-dressed man that he and Eli had seen in the woods the night before.

* * *

Abby never thought she'd be tired of hospitals, but she was—at least, she was tired of being a patient. Thankfully, she wasn't going to have to stay the night. The burns on her right arm were terribly painful, but the treatments done in the burn center and some pain medication had gotten them under control. She couldn't wait to get home and get cleaned up...that was, if Chief McClendon would let her go. She supposed she would find out soon enough. She'd been told he was sending two detectives to come talk to Blake and her in the hospital conference room.

She hoped Blake would return to the conference room soon. He had stayed with Abby until Dr. Dodd, the hospital administrator, had called him away for a meeting. Abby could only imagine that it had something to do with the whole crazy ordeal that seemed to be going on around them. But she wanted him there to clarify the events of the fire and those leading up to it when the police arrived.

"Miss Miller?"

"Yes?" Abby turned to a familiar face. It was the same detective who'd come to the hospital the other day with McClendon. "Oh, hello, Detective. Come on in and have a seat. Dr. Jamison should be back at any moment."

A tall brunette stood just behind him. "This is Agent Linda Day from the FBI. She's working this case and I'm her local liaison."

"Please, don't get up," Agent Day said. "I know you've had a rough week. You've certainly been keeping me busy."

The two officers took seats across from her.

"We have a few updates for you and then we want to hear about what happened at the Hall of Records today." Agent Day placed a tiny recording device on the table between them, then she opened up a leather notebook and took out a pen, ready to review and take notes.

"Sorry I'm late." Blake appeared at the door.

After introductions, Blake gave a quick rundown of exactly what had happened at the Hall of Records. Abby was surprised how much she had remembered accurately.

"Remarkable that you two escaped." Agent Day shook her head in disbelief. "According to the chief fire inspector, the inside hallway was the first to burn, the definite point of origin. Whoever set the fire used strong accelerants to draw the fire toward the document room, which, as you know, had only one exit. You were good and trapped. Everyone working the case is very impressed with your escape route."

"Except that it almost killed Abigail," Blake said. She could still hear the guilt in his voice.

"You might have both died if you hadn't gone into the crawl space," Agent Day replied. "You should be thankful, not critical."

Blake dropped his head. He seemed even more agitated since his return from meeting with Dr. Dodd.

"I heard you say that you have updates." Abby wanted to wrap up the meeting and get home. She wasn't sure if she could even take in any more information or warnings of danger. Exhaustion had set in days ago. Now even her fumes needed refueling. Soot and dirt covered every inch of her body. She needed a long, hot bath and an even hotter cup of tea.

"Yes." Agent Day turned to a different page in her notes. "Since this is my first meeting with you, I'm not sure where to start. I have no idea how much McClendon shared with you."

"Just tell us everything." Blake sighed.

Abby stiffened. Blake's presence both comforted her and disturbed her. She felt as if since their introduction in the E.R. a few days ago, they'd been together almost nonstop—and now that she thought about it, it had been nothing but nonstop trouble.

"Right," Agent Day said. "Well, then, here are the facts—Nicolas Hancock entered Fairview Hospital on Friday. He was given a lethal dose of epinephrine and died subsequently from cardiac arrest. We know virtually nothing about Mr. Hancock, except that he was a patient of a Dr. Granger, who is a family friend of Dr. Jamison's. Other than that, his contact information is bogus. His prints don't match anything in any of the databases, so he's not a criminal that we know of. Still, a man who uses an alias tends to raise eyebrows. The FBI has subpoenaed the medical records from Dr. Granger but we have so far been unable to identify Mr. Hancock. This is a problem because without knowing the victim, it's hard to put a finger on motive and therefore difficult to narrow in on possible suspects. We don't know how Hancock got to Fairview or who admitted him. Possibly it was the killer Miss Miller saw.

"Then Miss Miller was attacked at approximately the same time and suffered similar symptoms as Hancock. Miss Miller's home was broken into and her workspace was vandalized. The next day, Miss Miller was sideswiped and rear-ended on the way to her brother's by a black sedan, which was later spotted at Miller's Mill. Shortly before, Dr. Jamison was shot at while trying to connect with Mr. Linton. Today, the two of you were locked in the Hall of Records auxiliary building, from which you barely escaped when it went up in flames. The last two events are directly linked to Dr. Jamison's search for his birth parents. We think it's safe to assume that these events have all been sparked by Dr. Jamison's stay in Lancaster."

"So, the biggest missing piece is who Hancock is and why someone wanted him dead?" Abby asked.

"Yes. That and how Dr. Jamison's adoption is linked to

Hancock's murder. If someone just wanted Dr. Jamison out of Lancaster, then we don't think they would go to such extreme measures."

"It seems to me that's exactly what they want. And you may change your mind after you see this." Blake paused as he pulled a magazine from his lap. He opened it to a double-page spread in the front.

"What is it?" Abby felt her heart beat faster as she stood to better view the fancy magazine with its high-gloss pages. The section was titled *Updates*. Across the two pages were various pictures of men and women Abby assumed were New York socialites. Each picture was accompanied by a short paragraph explaining some sort of business deal or life event concerning each of the young men. One of the pictures was of Blake.

Abby read aloud.

"Not quite following in his parents' footsteps, Dr. Blake Jamison loses his first patient to a simple procedure while on a pro bono sabbatical in Lancaster County. Rumors have it that the cause is substance abuse. Speculations have been made that Dr. Jamison will not wield a scalpel much longer, either here or in the quaint countryside of PA.

"But this is ridiculous!" Abby said. "That patient was never in your care until after his cardiac arrest. By that point, he was beyond saving."

"It doesn't matter. Dr. Dodd has asked me to leave Fairview."

FOURTEEN

"Yes, Natalie." Blake held his cell phone about three inches from his ear. Natalie was so excited that the volume of her voice had increased enough to be heard by everyone in the small coffeehouse. "I can hear you. I just can't understand what you're saying."

"Saturday. The gala. Pick me up at six."

"Yeah, about that." Blake sighed. "I don't think—"

"You promised, Blake. You're making a toast and introducing the keynote speaker. You have to be there."

Guilt slinked around Blake's neck. Natalie was right. He'd agreed to this over a month ago. But that was before the murder and the bad publicity in the *New York Ways* magazine—and meeting Abigail. Still, he had to go back home. After talking with Agent Day, it seemed best for him to give up his search, leave the hospital, try to get that damaging article retracted and just get back to his regular life.

"You haven't seen this month's copy of *NYW,* have you?" Blake asked.

"*NYW?* No. No one has. It doesn't come out until next week. Why? Did you finally agree to do that cover story?"

Next week? Then how did Dr. Dodd have a copy of it already? "No, never mind. Look, Natalie. You're right. I should be there for the gala. I hope I *can* be there. Let me see if I can get things squared away down here by the end of the week. I'll talk to you in a couple of days."

He hung up. Well, that was interesting. Maybe he could get the story retracted before it actually hit the stands. Was that possible? He was afraid to hope.

Blake gulped down his last bit of espresso. It was no longer hot, but he wanted the shot of caffeine to keep him going. What were the chances of things getting wrapped up by the end of the week? Slim to none. Every time he hoped to get answers about what was going on, instead there only seemed to be new questions to add to the equation.

In fact, he could hardly keep track of all the questions. He wished his mother were still there to talk to. She always helped him to reason out things, especially when he had tough choices to make.

Blake left a generous tip for the waitress and slipped out of the coffeehouse. He drove to the bed-and-breakfast, ready to change into something a little nicer as Abby was meeting him there for dinner. Blake had not invited her. The Youngers, the owners of the bed-and-breakfast, had heard about the fire and insisted that they both come for a big dinner on the house.

Blake changed into khakis and a freshly starched oxford. Then he straightened up his room, caught up on email and sat down with the documents that Abby had saved from the Hall of Records fire.

Dr. Nathan Miles. Blake went back to his laptop and searched for the name on Google.

Ob-gyn. New York City.

What a surprise. In fact, Dr. Miles's practice was located at 73rd on the Upper East Side, just a few blocks from Blake's apartment.

Blake also looked up the *New York Ways* website. Natalie had been right, of course. This month's issue wasn't due out for a week. So, where had Dr. Dodd gotten his copy?

Blake studied the other birth notices, the ones with different dates but also with the Jane and John Doe mother and father listings. Could all five of those babies have been given up for adoption? Blake didn't know much about adoption rates, but he doubted that in a township as small as Willow Trace there were more than two or three a year. Not five in a three-week span, especially given what Abby had told him of how rare adoption was in the Amish community that made up much of the town.

Blake ran his hands through his hair. Nothing made sense. The only constant here was that everything seemed to point back to New York.

His hotel line rang. It was Mrs. Younger announcing Abby's arrival.

Blake put away the papers and shut down his laptop. He scurried down the steps but put on the brakes as he entered the dining room. His mouth went dry and his feet froze to the floor.

There was only one guest seated, facing him in the center of the room. She wore a knee-length pencil skirt with a fitted blouse. Her long blond hair was smoothed out and loose, falling over both shoulders and waving over the left half of her face. Blake thought his heart might leap from his chest. She was so beautiful.

"Wow, Abigail," he said. "Your—your hair… You should wear it down more often. It's incredible."

Her large blue eyes looked up at him with an awe-inspiring hypnotic effect. "Thank you. I haven't worn it this way since my *Rumschpringe* days. I felt so icky after that fire, I thought…why not dress up and look nice for a change? You know what I mean?"

Blake nodded. His hand missed the back of his chair as he reached to pull it out and take a seat.

"I hope you're okay with me coming to dinner." There was a natural blush on her cheeks. "It was so nice of the Youngers. They are a great couple."

Okay? He was more than okay. Abigail was already beautiful in the jeans and sweaters she wore, but with a skirt and blouse and her hair down, she would have given any runway model a run for her money.

"I'm glad you're here for dinner." Blake forced his eyes to his water glass, which he grabbed and nearly drained trying to relieve his dry mouth. "There are a few things I wanted to discuss with you."

One glance back into her mesmerizing blue eyes and he wasn't sure if he would be able to remember a single one of them. Blake shook his head. What was happening to him? Or had already happened…

"Me, too." Abigail swept her long hair behind her shoulder. It felt strange wearing it down. What would her father say?

She knew what the bishop would say…but he'd be wrong. She hadn't dressed this way to impress Blake. She'd done it because she'd spent too much time in the past few days covered in dirt or blood or both. The bed-and-breakfast had a nice restaurant, which made for a good excuse for dressing up—and this was the only fancy outfit she owned.

She looked down at the bandages that covered the burns on her arm. The pain was steady but bearable. Still, it fatigued her. She doubted very much that she would need to take the sleep aid the hospital had recommended.

"Well, there you are, Dr. Jamison." Mrs. Younger bounced into the room with a basket of hot yeast rolls, which she placed in the center of the table. "You can't keep a woman this special waiting. But I'm sure you already knew that."

Abby's cheeks were warm with a deep blush. She'd always liked the Youngers. Easy, no-nonsense Amish.

"Pop and I are very happy to take care of you both tonight," she continued. "It's going to be a special evening. Just sit back and enjoy. You don't even have to order. Pop already decided what the menu would be. First up is a bowl of hot Amish Church Soup. I'll be right back with that and some sweet tea. You must be starved after the rough time you've had these past few days."

Abby agreed. She was starved. And being in a fancy restaurant seemed to help put some distance between her and what had happened that afternoon.

"She's right. It has been a rough couple of days."

Blake nodded his agreement. "Yes, I was afraid you'd be too tired for this."

"What I'm too tired for is to cook for myself."

"Good point. So, how well do you know the Youngers? I really like them. They seem a bit different than your family, though—you know, in the way they are Amish."

"I went to school with their two daughters. You met Mary the other night. So I know them fairly well, but they belong to a different *Ordnung*. It's a little more modern than the one my family belongs to. And running the bed-and-breakfast and having *Englisch* guests all of the time…well, the Youngers have to be pretty in tune with everything on the outside. That makes them better hosts."

"They're the best. I'm really glad I decided to stay here." He looked down at her arms. "How much pain are you in?"

"It's okay. A steady, stinging burn, but nothing a good night's sleep won't fix."

"That was a close call. Your third one this week. Do you really think you'll be able to sleep well?"

"I hope so. I have a plan and I was hoping you'd be a part of it."

He smiled. "A plan? I like that. Let's hear it."

"Okay." Abby took a deep breath. "I hardly know where to start...." She smiled. "It has been a rough few days in more ways than one. And I'm ready to change all of that around. Like Eli has said from the beginning. We need to get ahead of this guy. I know this will surprise you but I've changed my mind about you finding your birth parents. I think you *should* find them. And I want to help. You said the very first day we met, when this whole thing started, that you didn't believe in coincidence. I don't, either."

Blake's dark-chocolate eyes softened as she spoke. "You're right. I'm surprised."

"Wait. There's more." Abby held up a hand. "I also want to get you reinstated at Fairview. And I think I know how to do that. What Dr. Dodd did today is completely unfair. He can't get away with it."

Mrs. Younger brought in the steaming soup and placed it before them. *"Guten appetiten."*

"Smells delicious," Blake said.

"It's Pop's Church Soup. He says it cures any ailment." She smiled. "Enjoy."

A few minutes of silence ensued as they plunged into their soup—steaming hot and loaded with richly stewed vegetables.

Blake put down his spoon and wiped his mouth with the cloth napkin. "I appreciate your sympathy. I agree about the situation. It doesn't seem too fair. But I don't know what can be done about it, unless we call a jury of peers. I don't want to do that. You saw the magazine today. After that hit to my reputation, I have to keep a low profile.

Anyway, Abby, I was going to tell you...I have decided to give up my search. It's gotten too dangerous. I have to go back to New York and take care of this article. Our foundations can't afford this bad publicity. You can't imagine what a mess it will start in New York if the wrong people get ahold of the information—it could ruin a lot of good organizations that my parents started. I really don't want that. You were right. My search is selfish and could bring a lot of pain to a lot of people. It already has."

Abby couldn't believe Blake had changed his mind. She had to talk him into continuing the search. It was the best way to get to the bottom of things. "What about the rest of the investigation? I think you must be close to finding your parents. You shouldn't give up now."

"I can't believe your change of heart." He looked truly bewildered. "I don't even know what to say." He swallowed hard. "It's been nothing but trouble since I came here. The fact that everything is tied back to New York, or seems to be, is what really has me convinced that I need to let it all go before someone else gets hurt."

"But that would only resolve half the problem." Abby sat tall in her chair. "You're forgetting that we witnessed a murder. Should we let the killer go free? And don't you care about getting reinstated? This is your career. I know you care about medicine. I saw you the other night helping Mrs. Brenneman. You are a great doctor."

"Thanks. I guess I hadn't had a chance for that to really sink in yet. I should call Dr. Dodd first thing in the morning. I was so stunned by that article, I didn't know how to respond. Speaking of which, I found out this afternoon that that article—the one I showed you and Agent Day—well, it hasn't been released yet. A friend of mine in New York said that magazine doesn't come out for another week. So how did Dr. Dodd get hold of a copy?"

Abby pressed her lips together. "That is strange. Can you keep it from coming out?"

"Maybe, but I'd need to get back to New York." He reached across the table and stroked her hand. "I wish things were different."

Abby knew what that meant. She pulled her hand away. Things weren't different, no matter what they might wish. Blake was engaged—and he was not her type, anyway. She could never understand the world he was from, much less be a part of it. "You're right. You should go back to New York."

He blinked hard. "I thought you just said I should stay and keep searching."

"I think you should do both. Go up to New York. Talk to Dr. Granger. Fix things at the magazine. And find some answers." Abigail focused her gaze on him, careful to remove any single romantic suggestion. "You said yourself, everything leads back to New York."

"And Dr. Miles."

"Dr. Miles?"

"Yes, the doctor whose name is on all those birth records. The ones you were so careful to save for me in the fire. Did you know that you also saved a letter from my mother? It's the last thing I have from her. You have no idea how much that letter means to me."

Abby could feel his eyes on her again. He did feel that connection between them, even though it could never amount to anything.

"I was going through those papers just a few minutes ago," Blake continued. "When I looked up Dr. Miles online, I found that he practices medicine in New York."

"That's just one more reason to go."

"Come with me."

"What? I can't go to New York."

"Here we are." Mrs. Younger bounced into the room again carrying a large tray. "Miller's Homemade Chicken Potpie. It's made from scratch, and all the ingredients are local and Amish grown."

"Miller? As in Abigail Miller?" Blake looked over at her.

Mrs. Younger explained as she placed the plates on the table with pride. "Oh, yes, it's the best recipe there is. I had to beg for it, but Abigail's mother finally relented after I told her that we didn't want our tourists going away not knowing who started the chicken potpie. Of course, Abby and her mother make it best, but I hope you'll both find this a close second. In any case, it's the best comfort food in the world."

"I don't know about you," Abby said after Mrs. Younger had left them alone, "but I could use a little comfort."

"No kidding." Blake smiled before digging into his pie. "Wow. That's the best chicken potpie I've ever had. And you can make it better? I think I'd like to try that."

Abby blushed and looked away. It had been so long since she'd cooked with her mother. So long since she'd thought about caring for someone in that way. There was something intimate and loving about making food for the people you cared for. Blake's comments forced up a longing in her that she'd put away years ago when she'd decided to become a nurse.

Abby forced down a bite of the chicken pie. It was full of familiar home-cooked flavors but they gave her no comfort just now. She had to help Blake, because that was the only way this whole ordeal would end. He was really starting to get under her skin and it scared her. She did not want to feel this way. And she certainly didn't want to feel this way about someone like Blake.

"I don't really cook anymore," she said. "But I could

give you the recipe. Maybe you could have your private chef make it for you."

Blake laughed at her teasing tone. "Seriously. It's not like that. No private chef for me."

"So you cook?"

"I eat out." He smiled. "Come to New York with me tomorrow. We've been in this whole ordeal together, it doesn't seem right if I go alone, especially if I end up getting some answers from Dr. Miles. You deserve to be the first to know."

"Dr. Jamison, I'm so sorry. We're both so sorry." Mr. and Mrs. Younger raced into the dining room half-breathless. "I must have left the back doors open. I can't believe it."

Abby put down her fork. "What is it? You both look pale as sheets."

"I was just going in to give you fresh towels for the night and turn down your bed...." Mrs. Younger shook her head. "You're so meticulously neat. I knew you couldn't have left your room like that."

"Someone's been in my room?" Blake stood.

Mr. and Mrs. Younger both looked down, nodding their heads nervously.

"It's terrible." Mrs. Younger looked as if she might cry. "They've ruined everything. I'm so sorry."

FIFTEEN

Blake stood at the doorway of his hotel room and scanned the wreckage. Every word the Youngers had said was true. Clothes had been strewn everywhere. Anything and everything of value had been taken—his watch, his computer, and the precious file containing the newly found birth records and the letter from his mother.

Chief McClendon and Detective Langer shook their heads as they surveyed the space. As with the hospital, Abby's car wreck and the break-in at her clinic, the FBI investigative team, headed by Agent Day, took pictures and asked lots of questions.

Blake was not just tired this evening; this event had made him angry.

"How can we end this?" he heard Abby murmuring to one of the agents. He couldn't have agreed more. And he realized that everything she'd been saying at dinner was right. He needed to go to New York to see if they could connect the dots. At least it was worth a try.

He pulled Detective Langer aside and told him that he planned to go to the city in the morning and that he hoped Abby would go with him. Langer explained that he or someone from the FBI might accompany them. He would look into it and get back to Blake as soon as possible. In any case, they weren't to go anywhere for the night. Langer and Day wanted them both to stay at the bed-and-breakfast.

"It's safe to have you in one place, where we can be certain you're protected," Agent Day explained. "The Youngers have rooms for each of you. One of the FBI agents is going to take one of the other rooms. You should both sleep well."

Abby wrapped her arms around her chest. He supposed it was to stop her shivering. She looked on the verge of tears. She was clearly not happy about having to stay the night there. "You'll have to get word to my brother. He's expecting me."

"Should I tell him you're going to New York tomorrow?" Langer asked her.

Her eyes shot a surprised look to Blake and he nodded. "You were right. I thought we could go up for the day... talk to Granger and Miles and someone at the magazine. Maybe we'll learn something."

Abby nodded to Langer. Blake was glad. He wanted her to be with him when he talked to the people in New York. Somehow he felt it would be helpful—or maybe he just liked the idea of her being by his side. Although tonight, she looked so weak and frail—she was not the spunky woman who was just having a nice dinner with him. Part of him wanted to put an arm around her and pull her close. It was getting harder for him to look at her and not feel the strong pull of the attraction and admiration for her that had developed over the past few days.

Ignoring those feelings, as he knew he had to do, Blake took hold of her hurt arm and lifted one of the bandages. "I need to change this dressing. Come on."

She looked up at him with her dark blue eyes, which began to smile back at him. "I'm sorry about all your things getting stolen. Especially the letter from your mother."

The understanding in her words touched him deeply and caused a lump to form in his throat. He had to look away as he swallowed it down and led her away to tend to her burn.

"Is this truly your first trip to the city?" Blake asked as he steered his Land Rover through the Holland Tunnel into Manhattan.

"First time out of Pennsylvania." Abby couldn't believe she'd slept almost the entire way to New York. But at least she was feeling better. The lump on her head was gone. The burns on her arms had stopped hurting. Her energy was returning. "I've been to Philly once but other than that I haven't been outside of Lancaster. I guess that's hard for you to imagine. You've been all over the world."

Blake shrugged and grinned at her. He looked well rested and extremely handsome in a pair of gray dress slacks with a yellow oxford. She liked how he rolled the sleeves up, making it easy to see the strong muscles of his forearms.

"What about high school and college? You must have left home for that."

"But I didn't go far. I was homeschooled with a Mennonite family that lives close to my parents. My dad gave me until I was twenty for education, which was very generous. So I finished high school at sixteen and commuted to a small college. I was a registered nurse by age nineteen."

"That's impressive," Blake said. "And it's great your parents gave you and your brother choices and opportunities."

"I think now my *dat* wishes he hadn't. He thinks he failed as a father—as an Amish father, that is."

"It's ironic, actually, that my parents weren't as liberal with me as yours were with you and your brother. I wasn't given choices. I had to have what they thought was the best whether it was what I wanted or not."

There was sadness not bitterness in his voice.

"Do you think that you would have chosen differently?"

"I don't know. I hadn't really thought about it until they died. It was then I realized that I had everything. Always, I've had everything—and yet, no peace."

"We find our peace in God," Abby said.

"That I know, thanks to my nanny. She made sure I understood the love of God. I do get that, Abby." Blake pressed his lips together. "I have spiritual peace. I just don't always like who I am, what I do, where I live, my friends."

Abby didn't have time to consider his words too much as they drove down an elegant street lined with designer shops and fancy restaurants.

"This is the Upper East Side. I grew up here."

"You don't like this?" she asked rhetorically. "Really?"

Such beautiful homes and stylish apartment buildings. Even the well-dressed and coiffed pedestrians looked as if they'd come straight out of a magazine—a magazine like the one Blake had shown her the other day. Abby grew more and more uncomfortable by the minute. "I guess I see what you mean by having the best. Poor you...."

"I know. That's why I've never said to anyone what I just said to you. I should be nothing but grateful. And I am. But I sometimes wonder what I would have been or what I would have done if I had made more of my own choices. That's all. I'm not ungrateful. Or disappointed. I just want to find that peace inside again and know I'm exactly where God wants me to be."

There was a struggle in his expression Abby had never seen before. Blake wasn't merely looking for his birth parents. He was looking for himself. He just didn't know it yet.

"Dr. Granger's office is just around the corner. We'll

park here. I called ahead to let them know I'd be coming in today."

"Is this your office here?"

"No, but my apartment is. I thought we'd park here and take cabs." Blake turned down an alley and stopped in front of a hidden garage door. He pressed a button on his dash and the door disappeared slowly into the wall. Inside was underground parking. An armed guard sat in a small glassed-in office. He looked up and waved to Blake, who smiled back and drove straight to a corner spot, crowned with a sign on the wall that read Dr. Jamison in large black letters. Almost every other spot was occupied—occupied by cars that Abby knew cost more than she could earn in two years.

Blake gave a half laugh. "Funny. It feels like I've been away for ages. Not a week."

He turned off the car and looked over at her. He reached across the console and touched her forearm. "Thank you."

"For what?" She slid her arm away and glanced in another direction. He had no idea how uncomfortable he made her.

He smiled. "I don't know. For being here. For being you."

She looked back at him. "I just want us both to be able to get on with our lives."

"Abby, are you ever afraid you're going to let everyone down?"

"Sure. All the time. And I have. Look at my father. I couldn't have let him any more down if I'd tried."

"Do you think you'll go back to what he wants for you? Get married? Be what your father thinks you should be?" His eyes were warm like chocolate and the meaning behind his question went beyond her conflict with her father.

He was asking her what she saw for her future. Would it be Amish? Or *Englisch?*

She shook her head, filled with sad emotions. She didn't want to care about Blake the way she was starting to. Nothing could be more stupid. But he felt it, too. She could see it in his eyes. She had to put an end to his hope once and for all.

"No. I won't go back. And I won't get married. I'll keep living the life I have now—the one I've chosen. That's where I belong. But I hope one day my father will want me just the way I am."

There was silence as she followed Blake out of the parking garage and down 73rd Street.

"Dr. Granger, thank you so much for taking the time to see us this morning on such short notice." Blake shook the elderly doctor's hand and introduced him to Abigail.

"Your parents were such dear friends to Stella and me. You know you are welcome anytime." He motioned for them to take a seat in the chairs on the other side of his desk. "Would you like a coffee or tea?"

After they declined, he excused his assistant and took a seat in a big leather chair behind his desk. "How can I help you, Blake? Miss Miller?"

Blake first explained about his sabbatical to Lancaster, which Dr. Granger had little reaction to. "Abigail and I both saw this patient and his paperwork. His name was Hancock, Nicolas Hancock. His file indicated that he'd been your patient at Norcross Hospital before being transferred to Fairview. Then Mr. Hancock died, and some…irregularities were found in his information. Enough to make the police believe he might have a different identity completely. It's put me in a bit of a situation with Fairview. I thought if you had any particular information you could pass on about him, it might be helpful."

Dr. Granger leaned forward, his expression flat as he made a steeple with his fingertips over the desk in front of him. "A police detective was here just a few days ago, asking similar questions. I'll have to tell you the same thing I told him. Any client information is privileged, as you both know. I can't divulge anything to any of you. I'm very sorry."

"I don't think that confidentiality applies here." Blake was ready for his response, even though he'd hoped to hear a different one. "You were his physician and so was I, according to the transfer chart. Any information you pass on to me is a consultation over a common patient. That is completely legal."

Dr. Granger frowned. He sat upright and shifted his weight, again clearly thinking over his answer before speaking. He raised a hand and pressed a speaker button on his phone. "Mrs. Timmons, could you please bring me the Nicolas Hancock file?"

Almost instantly, Mrs. Timmons rushed in with a thin patient file. She passed it over the desk to Dr. Granger. He opened it, looked inside and closed it again before smiling at Mrs. Timmons. "Thank you. Please close the door on your way out."

Mrs. Timmons left the room and Dr. Granger passed over the file to Blake. "I'll let you thumb through it. I'm afraid I can't give you a copy without consulting my lawyer. I'm sorry, Blake. I wish I could be more forthcoming, especially to you, but as you know with malpractice suits running rampant, I just can't be too cautious."

"I understand. I appreciate this." Blake reached a nervous hand over and took the file. He opened it and began to scan the first page.

"Well, then…I hope that helps you both. Now if you'll excuse me, I have patients waiting. Please take your time. Mrs. Timmons will see you out and you can leave the folder with her." He shook Blake's hand as he passed on his way out of the office. "A pleasure to see you again, Blake. I hope this situation at Fairview is resolved quickly. Miss Miller, lovely to meet you."

"Dr. Granger?" Blake stood and turned to the door. The old friend of his parents' looked back over his shoulder. "Did my parents ever tell you that I was adopted?"

Dr. Granger stopped fast. His shoulders rose up as he took in a quick breath. He turned his head back slowly. He was still smiling but the expression was different than it had been earlier. "No. I didn't know that. In fact, I find that hard to believe. How did you find out about this?"

"My mother told me."

"Well…as I said, that surprises me, Blake." Granger was frowning now. "If I were you, I'd be careful who I shared that with."

"Oh, I am, Doctor. I am very careful." Blake watched Granger leave the room. Then he tossed the Hancock file on the desk and turned to Abby. "Come on. Let's go."

"Don't you want to read the file?"

"No, it's a phony. Dr. Granger was lying about almost everything."

SIXTEEN

"How do you know he was lying?" Abby asked as they sped along in a cab toward the magazine office. She didn't question for a moment whether Blake was right or not. She hadn't liked Dr. Granger. There was something slightly snaky about his expressions. And she didn't appreciate how he'd added that ominous warning to Blake after he inquired about the adoption.

"It was obvious that he was lying about not knowing I was adopted. Dr. Granger used to work with my mother. How could he not have known? All of a sudden his colleague has a baby and was never pregnant?"

"So why lie about it to you now that you already know?"

Blake shrugged. "I can't imagine why he was lying at all. Just like I can't imagine why he would go to all the trouble to create a phony Hancock folder. It was so generic—and the specifics were dead wrong. Said the man was six feet tall and had blond hair."

"He was bald and maybe five foot eight."

"Exactly."

"It's like he was expecting us or expecting the detective to return with a warrant for the file." Abby sighed. "Maybe the visit to the magazine publishing offices will be more productive."

"I'm not so sure that this visit wasn't advantageous. The clock has been ticking ever since we saw Hancock and now it's ticking double-time. I think we are closing in on things. Just one little missing piece will have it all make sense."

"Or one big piece," Abby said with a teasing tone.

"Yes. And here we are. This is what they call midtown."

Abby could hardly believe the size of the buildings. It hurt her neck to look up at them. They exited the cab and stood together in front of the giant publishing company.

"Wow. You know, you can't really fathom how so many people can be on one little island until you get here and see it for yourself. Are you sure Langer is still behind us? I don't see how he can keep up with all this traffic and people. It's amazing."

"He's right there." Blake nodded his head in the direction of the other side of the street. The Lancaster detective was leaning against a park bench with a newspaper rolled up under his arm—his eyes on the two of them.

Blake opened the front doors of the fifty-plus-story building on Avenue of the Americas. "*New York Ways* offices are on the twenty-eighth floor."

After passing through a tight security check, a bellman ushered them up to the magazine offices and helped to buzz them inside. Blake told the receptionist who he was and that he wanted to see the managing editor, Mitchell Bain.

For ten minutes, Abby and Blake pretended to look through back issues. As fate would have it, Abby picked up an issue containing the same photo she'd seen of Blake and Natalie, with the caption about their upcoming engagement. She turned the magazine around and showed him, hoping her expression was pleasant, hiding the lump that had lodged in her throat.

Blake groaned, taking the magazine from her hands.

"I remember that. That's the day Daveux practically accosted me."

"And your fiancée?" Abby bit her lip at her own catty remark. *Way to hide the feelings, Abigail.*

"She's *not* my fiancée. She was," Blake said, passing the photo back to her with an annoyed expression. He stared her square in the eyes. "But I called it off because it would have been the biggest mistake of my life."

Who was he trying to convince—her or himself?

"It's none of my business," Abby said.

Blake had just opened his mouth to reply when Mr. Bain walked into the reception area.

"Dr. Jamison! I hope you're here to say that you're finally agreeing to a cover story." Bain's voice was overbearingly loud and almost comical coming from such a small man. His suit was made of expensive material but in a very loud pattern, and his tie had been loosened at the neck with the top few buttons of his shirt open, revealing a thick gold chain.

"Not exactly." Blake stood and motioned to Abby. "This is Abigail Miller. We work together at the hospital."

"Ms. Miller, nice to meet you." Bain looked tense and his speech was hurried. "Well, then…if you're not here about a cover story, then what can I do for you today?"

"If we could speak somewhere privately?" Blake suggested politely.

Blake and Abby followed Bain down a long, narrow hallway lined with closet-size offices, most occupied by severely stressed-looking men and women busy typing away at their computers. At the end of the hallway, they entered a slightly larger office where they took seats around Bain's tiny desk. He had to remove a few stacks of papers so that they could all see each other. He sat back, glancing down at the screen of his smartphone as he waited for Blake to speak.

"First of all, I want to know how you got this story. And then how it got to a Dr. Dodd at Fairview Hospital." Blake handed over the magazine copy that he'd gotten from Dr. Dodd—the one with the short blurb about Hancock's death, which insinuated malpractice in the affair.

Bain took the copy from Blake. His stubby fingers reminded Abby of her attack at the hospital. She closed her eyes against the flash of images firing through her mind, but she couldn't stop them. The fat fingers closing around her arm. She could still feel the bruise on her flesh even now. And those cold gray eyes...

"I don't know who Dr. Dodd is and I certainly don't know how this got to anyone." Bain turned page after page of the magazine issue with an astonished look on his face. "This hasn't come out and I didn't authorize this blurb about you. I'm as stunned as you are, Dr. Jamison. In fact, I have the mock-up for this month's issue right here. It releases next week, so of course it's already been finalized, but you aren't in it. This page is completely different."

While Bain pulled the mock-up of the current issue up on his computer, Blake looked over at Abigail. "The missing piece?"

She nodded. "One of them."

Bain showed them the current issue, which—as he'd said—did not include the small but damaging paragraph about Blake, Hancock's death and Fairview Hospital.

"So, how could a doctor in Lancaster produce a magazine copy so convincing and with every other page of the issue exactly correct?" Abby asked.

"It had to come off our printer, I suppose? Or maybe someone here on staff?" Bain said. "But it's completely against policy. Staff members are not even allowed to discuss articles, let alone distribute early copies or, even worse, tampered copies. I want to know who is responsible for this. This is exactly the kind of employee that will sell me out to the *New Yorker* and put me out of business."

"Who usually writes these blurbs for you?" Blake asked.

"Freelance writers," Bain said. "There's one in particular that sort of comes and goes. A photojournalist. I can't think of his name. I haven't heard from him in weeks. I don't like him. He writes a good story but he always goes too far. The *NYW* is about showing successes in New York. Not this." He threw the phony magazine on the desk. "I'll do anything you need, Dr. Jamison, to find the person responsible. I intend to get to the bottom of this."

Abby leaned forward. "How about you start by calling Dr. Dodd and telling him what you just told us so that Dr. Jamison can get back to work at the hospital?"

Bain nodded. "Done. What else?"

"The name of the writer you're talking about..." Abby said. "It doesn't happen to be Daveux, does it?"

"Yes. That's it. Phillipe Daveux." Bain hit the top of the magazine copy with his hand. "This is exactly the sort of thing he likes to dig up. And if not him, one of the others in his little club, as we call it. You know they all hang together—that group of journalists and photographers."

Abby and Blake exchanged glances.

"So, it might be worth our while to speak to him or to this group," Blake said.

"I suppose. But I can assure you that copy will not be hitting the newsstands."

"I'd still like to know how he got the information, if he is the one responsible," Blake said. "Are you allowed to give us his contact information?"

"Daveux is not his real name. Let me check with Payroll."

Bain picked up his phone and called Payroll. Seconds later, Bain checked his computer. "Payroll is going to email the information.... Ah, here it is. Lyle Morris."

"Lyle Morris?"

"Right. Daveux is an alias," Bain explained. "You know, a pen name. These guys dig up dirt on people like you but they don't want you doing the same. They all use fake names to protect themselves and their families. So, do you want his info?"

Blake typed the address and phone number into his phone. They would have to work in another visit during their trip.

"Thank you, Mr. Bain. You've been extremely helpful."

"What do you say we grab a bite before we go see Dr. Miles? This is one of my favorites." Blake had the taxi stop in front of an elegant bistro.

"I'd say I thought you'd never ask. I'm famished. Also, we should probably let Langer know our additional plans, right?"

"We should."

Blake was immediately greeted by the maître d' of the little French restaurant, who made a little more fuss over him than was necessary. They sat, ordered and called Langer.

"Well, look who's back in town and doesn't call his friends?" A foursome of young men surrounded their table.

"How's that country-doctor thing working out for you?" another of the men asked.

Blake smiled with reserve. "Abby, meet my partners. This is Bill, Sam, Devin and Artie."

"Nice to meet you."

"Nice to meet you, too," the one named Artie said,

making big eyes. "Are you the reason Jamison took off to the country?"

"I don't think so."

"Abby is a nurse at Fairview Hospital. We're here checking on a patient." Blake ignored their efforts to belittle his sabbatical.

"Kind of a long-distance house visit."

"Blake, you really need to look over all those files I sent you. The lawyer and business manager are tired of waiting."

"I'll get to it as soon as possible," Blake said.

The others nodded, but even Abby could feel their frustration with Blake. If only they knew what he'd been through over the past few days, but she imagined they had no idea.

"Well," one of them said as they moved away, "if you're here tonight, a group of us are meeting up at the club after work. You should both come."

"Thanks, but we're not staying." Blake shook his head. "Like I said, we are here on hospital business and have to get back to Lancaster tonight."

His partners' faces expressed mixtures of bewilderment, concern and perhaps even some amusement.

When they had gone, Blake sat down again and placed his napkin in his lap. "Sorry about those guys. They aren't too on board with my sabbatical to Fairview."

Their sandwiches came quickly and Abby found that she was even hungrier than she'd thought. Getting some food into her system seemed to recharge her spirits, too. What did she care if Blake was a rich New York doctor with lots of rich, good-looking friends? They just needed to find out what had happened back at Fairview so they could both get on with their lives.

She took a long drink of water, thinking over all the events of the past few days.

"You asked me what I'll ask Daveux…. I guess the most important thing to get out of him is whether or not he knows how that information about Hancock's death got to the magazine."

"What?" Abby was still staring out the window, lost in her own review of the events, not listening. "I'm sorry. I was just thinking all that over. You know, we know why I'm a target. But why are you a target? Why does someone want you away from Fairview so badly? Maybe the information you need about your birth parents is at the hospital."

Blake scratched his head. "I hadn't thought about that. Maybe I should talk to Dr. Dodd?"

"Maybe…"

"Maybe?" Blake followed her eyes to the front desk, where the maître d' pointed a long-legged brunette dressed in a gorgeous black fitted suit toward them.

"Natalie?"

"Yes. I'd bet a million dollars one of my partners thought this would be funny."

Abby shrugged. "I'll just go powder my nose and give you a few minutes alone."

She started to stand but Blake grabbed her by the arm. He clamped his fingers on her tiny wrist and gently kept her from pulling away. Natalie was quickly approaching. Abby hated that her heart was beating so fast. She hoped Blake couldn't tell what she felt inside. That he mattered to her. And that she was so happy that this woman was no longer his fiancée. Of course, what, then, was Natalie to him? And why was she here hunting him down?

SEVENTEEN

"Sit down, Abby." Blake looked at her with pleading brown eyes. "Please? You don't need to go powder anything. You need to stay right here. With me."

Blake tried to silently plead with Abby to stay in her seat.

"Please?"

Abby sat back in her seat with reluctance.

"There you are." Natalie stopped beside the table. Her eyes dropped down to where Blake held tight to Abigail's hand. Her perfectly toned skin blanched.

"I suppose Artie told you we were here?" he said.

"He said *you* were here with a colleague."

"Good old Artie."

"Hi, I'm Abigail Miller. I work at the hospital where Blake is on sabbatical." Abby wriggled her arm free and offered her hand to Natalie.

Natalie shook Abby's hand but not without giving her the up and down. Abby slyly contained a smile at Natalie's shallow behavior.

"So, here on business and you didn't even call?"

"Why would I call you, Natalie?"

"We have a lot to go over for the gala." She looked behind her, grabbed an empty chair and made a place for herself at the table. "We could talk now, if Miss Miller doesn't mind?"

Abby shrugged. "Sure."

"I mind." Blake stood. He walked around Natalie and reached his arm around Abigail. "We have a two-o'clock appointment. I know this is short notice and I'm sorry for that, but I may not make it to the gala, Nat. You should ask someone else to introduce the keynote speaker."

"What?" She stood as they walked away. "What about the foundation? Your parents? What will everyone say? You have responsibilities, Blake. You can't just move to Tombouctou and think that everything you left behind will just take care of itself."

Blake stopped. He looked at Abigail. He'd felt more peace with her in a week and with a killer after them than he'd ever had in New York City with Natalie and everything in the world at his fingertips. And yet, Natalie was right. He had responsibilities. He owed it to his parents to run the foundation and continue their work. Was there a way he could do that without falling into the trap of his old life?

"Don't move," he said to Abby. "Stay right here. Promise me."

"And miss this? Are you kidding?" She smiled. But he knew Abby was uncomfortable and confused about his friendship with Natalie. If only he'd fully explained it before…

Blake sighed as he walked back to Natalie. "You're right, Natalie. I do want to slip from these responsibilities for a bit. In fact, I have to. I have some things I have to figure out and I'm asking you as a friend to try to understand that."

She looked over his shoulder at Abby. "Is she what you're trying to figure out?"

He glanced back at Abigail, too. "Look, Nat, just cover for me at the gala. After that, I'll get back to work with the foundation."

"Then you're coming back from Pennsylvania?" Natalie lit up.

"I don't know."

"Are you in love with her?" Natalie frowned disapprovingly. "She's so...plain."

"Goodbye, Nat. Thanks for taking care of the gala." Blake walked back to Abigail. "We need to hurry to Dr. Miles's office. It's not in this part of town."

He hailed a cab and followed Abby into it. "I'm sorry about all that back there."

"All what? I told you before it's none of my business." Abby looked him square in the eyes. She was either really put off with him or she meant exactly what she said. Either way, he didn't like it one bit. As soon as there was a chance, he was going to tell her the whole story, whether she wanted to hear it or not.

"You know, I haven't seen Langer since we went into the restaurant. Should we be worried?"

"No. He knows our agenda." They exited the cab in SoHo near St. John's Park and began to walk the three blocks east to Miles's office.

"Is that Langer?" Abby motioned toward a man standing outside of a deli just across the street.

"I can't tell—he has his head down. But he had this address, so that would make sense that he..."

"What?" Abby asked him. "You look concerned."

"I just thought I saw..." *Dr. Granger.* "Never mind. My eyes are playing tricks on me. You know, Abigail, you can ask me anything about my friends, including Natalie. Or about my life in New York. I can't help but notice that you seem a little tense after lunch. I hope that wasn't because of the unexpected interruptions."

"I—I don't have any questions, Blake. I'm tense because we're in trouble and the detective assigned to escort us seems to be missing." She looked at him with a matter-of-fact expression.

Blake dropped his head as he opened the door to Dr. Miles's office. Apparently, she really didn't care about him or his life here. And what did it matter? He had to come back to New York, back to his practice and back to the foundation. He owed it to his parents, and besides, it was important, valuable work.

Even if it could never make him fully happy.

Abby pushed away all thoughts of Blake's offer to ask him questions about his life in New York. She'd seen plenty with her own two eyes. Now she just needed to figure this mystery out and get back to her clinic.

Dr. Miles's office was warm and cozy, painted brightly in shades of orange and yellow. Three women in their second or third trimesters sat in the waiting room, reading on Kindles and iPads. Abby felt comforted by the scene—finally, something familiar to her, when the rest of New York had seemed like a foreign planet. A young and attractive nurse escorted them to a small office. They sat opposite the desk and Dr. Miles joined them in less than a minute. He was a big, white-headed and white-bearded man, jovial and handsome. He could have played Santa Claus at Macy's without even applying any makeup. He even had a deep, jolly chuckle and a twinkle in his eye. All he lacked was the red suit. It made him seem familiar and Abby couldn't help but think that she must have met him before.

"Dr. Miles," Blake said after introducing the two of

them. "I understand that about thirty years ago you were working in Lancaster County?"

His eyes opened wide but his smile never faltered. "That's right. I wasn't there for long. Just my first year out of medical school."

"Do you remember delivering babies for any Amish families?"

"Well, yes. Yes, I do. Many."

"Were any of those babies put up for adoption that you know of?"

He chuckled again and smiled wider. "That was a long time ago, son. But I don't remember any. Of course, I'm not so sure I'd know about an adoption. I just went in and delivered the baby. I worked nights on call. I hardly knew the patients. I never saw the families after the babies were born. I wasn't the main doctor. Just his night watchman, so to speak."

"So, who was the main obstetrician for the practice?" Abby asked.

Dr. Miles dropped his smile for a nanosecond, recovering his cheery disposition with another one of his chuckles. "It was a large practice. There were many others. I don't remember all their names. So, why all the questions about my early career? I guess I misunderstood why you needed to see me. What exactly is this all about?"

Blake cleared his throat. "We work at Fairview Hospital in Lancaster and we're trying to straighten up some incomplete birth files. Your name or your signature is on many of these incomplete records. I know it was a long time ago, but we were just hoping you might remember if some of the babies you delivered ended up going out for adoption. Several of these birth records you signed have Jane and John Doe listed as the parents."

Once more, Dr. Miles's eyes flickered and his jovial

Santa Claus demeanor slipped away. This time, a sense of evil flashed across his face. Abby closed her eyes. Could it be? Could those gray Santa Claus eyes be the same ones that delivered a lethal injection to her arm? The voice sounded like the one she'd heard in that hallway— but was her mind playing tricks on her, making her think she was hearing similarities that weren't actually there? Abby's fingers tightened around the arms of her chair as she tried to remain calm.

"Did the hospital send you here?" Dr. Miles asked, his composure now completely returned.

"No, sir. This is more of a personal quest."

"I see. Well, I may be able to help you." He stood and pulled a buzzing pager from his waist. He turned his head away from them and Abby could no longer double-check his face for comparison with the doctor she'd walked in on in the closed-off wing of Fairview.

"Stay here," he said. "I have some old files stacked away in storage. I'll be right back." He slipped out, shutting the door to his office behind him.

Blake was so frustrated he didn't notice her shaking and still, seated in her chair. "Well, that was a waste of time. I'm afraid we aren't going to get anything from Daveux, either. And this whole trip will have been useless."

"Check the door," she said.

"What?" Blake turned to her and lifted an eyebrow. "Abby, what's the matter? You're shaking from head to toe."

"Dr. Miles, I think he's the same doctor I—I saw... I think he's the same doctor that—"

Blake put a hand on her trembling shoulder. "Shh."

"Try the door."

Blake put his hand on the knob. It wouldn't turn. "He locked us in?"

"He locked us in. Of course he locked us in. He's a killer!"

"Hold on," Blake said, pulling a credit card from his wallet.

"You really think that will work?" Abby asked.

"I hope so." Blake inserted the card through the crack between the door and the doorframe. He pulled it down and wiggled the doorknob. Abby held her breath.

Click!

It worked. Blake pushed the door open, grabbed Abby by the hand and raced out of the room. At the end of the hallway was a fire-exit stairwell. They ran for it and dashed out of the hallway as fast as they could. With his free hand, Blake dialed Detective Langer. "We're coming out of the building. Pick us up!"

EIGHTEEN

"Whew! That was close."

A few minutes later, they were safe inside an unmarked police vehicle and talking on the phone to Agent Day.

"It was him. I'm sure of it." Abby clutched the phone in her shaking hands. "Dr. Miles, he was the man with Hancock in the empty wing of Fairview. He's the one who killed Hancock and then tried to kill me. He hid it at first with his phony smiles and jovial attitude, but the second he became angry, his eyes gave him away."

"Okay. Okay." Blake could hear Day's voice over the line loud and clear. "I'll get our people on that angle. He wasn't even on our radar but we will definitely look into it ASAP. We've been so busy focusing on the doctors at the hospital and Granger that we hadn't—"

"Tell her that Miles may have worked at Fairview at one time—or at least that he worked for people who worked at the hospital. He said so himself. That would have been thirty years ago, but he'd still know his way around the building."

Abby nodded and passed on the information. After a few more of Day's questions, she disconnected and put the phone away. Langer was taking them to the address for Philippe Daveux, aka Lyle Morris—their last visit of the day.

"Are you sure you're up for this visit to Mr. Morris?" Blake asked. "I'm sure you could sit with Langer while I go to the apartment."

"No way. I want to go with you. I want to see this guy who prints lies and tries to ruin other people's lives."

The drive to the apartment was a long one, all the way to the Upper West Side. Even Blake was surprised to find that the address took them to a lovely brownstone not too far from Central Park.

"I suppose writing freelance articles is a pretty good living," Blake said. After a nod to Langer, he followed Abby up the front steps, joining her just as she rang the doorbell. Footsteps sounded up to the front door, which slowly cracked open but only as far as the chain lock would allow.

"Mrs. Morris?" Blake said.

"Who's asking?" The woman was a caramel blonde, mid-forties with large dark circles under her eyes as if she'd been sick for a long time. Her accent was thick, French, perhaps.

"I'm Abigail Miller and this is Dr. Blake Jamison." Abby stepped forward, thinking she might be a little less intimidating to the woman than Blake in his stiff, starched shirt. "We just came from *New York Way* magazine after talking to the managing editor, Mr. Bain. There's a really important article we'd like to discuss with Lyle Morris. We tried his cell phone and couldn't get an answer."

The woman let her words sink in. She looked at Blake. "You look familiar, *non?*"

"Yes," Blake said. "Your...husband? Mr. Morris has written a few articles about my family."

Mrs. Morris hesitated again, her eyes stuck on Blake. At length, she shut the door, unfastened the chain lock and reopened it. "I don't know what to tell you. Lyle left last week to follow a story. I haven't heard from him since. I thought he would be back by now. Maybe tomorrow he will be here. I don't know. If you want to leave your number, I can have him call you when he returns."

"This really can't wait." Blake pressed her. "You must have some way to get in touch with him. In case of an emergency?"

"I don't." She shrugged. "He doesn't like to be bothered while he's working. And we are all fine here, as you see."

Abby scratched her head, unable to understand the arrangement the Morrises seemed to have. "Do you know what sort of story he was working on? This is really important. Dr. Jamison's foundation for children with medical needs and his own career are at risk. If you can help us…"

"I only know that he was traveling." She tilted her head to the side. "So this story you want to talk to him about— it is about you, Dr. Jamison? I know about your foundation. My husband and I, of course, have great interest in it. Our oldest son was born with a birth defect. Your foundation funded a special operation for him that our insurance would not pay."

No wonder the man had devoted a webpage to Blake and his family and written so many articles about the foundation. He was personally invested in it.

"I would love to hear his story," Blake said.

Again, the woman hesitated, but then she stepped aside and motioned for them to come in.

They followed Mrs. Morris down a narrow hallway lined with amazing black-and-white photos in simple gray frames.

"Your husband took these?"

"Yes."

"He is very talented."

"But this work does not bring money. Everyone, they want a scandal. Everyone wants to read about someone else's dirt. I do not understand this. But I am not American."

"Well, I am American," said Abby. "And I don't understand it, either."

"Here. Have a seat. I'll look at Lyle's desk calendar. If there are any notes about where he might be, they would be there." Mrs. Morris gestured to a small brown couch.

The living space was cramped with overstuffed furniture and more framed black-and-white photos. "Are these your sons?"

"Yes. Freddy and Nate. They are at school." Mrs. Morris scooted behind the couch to a hidden alcove.

Abby continued to study the images of the boys that were hung all along the opposing wall. Blake, too, seemed fixated on a set of photographs—another series that was displayed neatly across the end table on his side of the sofa.

They could hear her riffling through files and papers on her husband's desk. "I don't see anything…. Wait… here is something…maybe…"

While Mrs. Morris spoke, Blake's hand reached back and took hold of Abby's wrist.

"I think I know where Lyle Morris is." He turned his head to her and spoke in the lowest whisper.

"Where?" Abby's eyes grew wide.

"In the morgue." Blake pulled one of the small photos off the side table and handed it to her.

Abby shivered as she recognized the round, bald-headed face of Nicolas Hancock. No wonder Mrs. Morris hadn't heard from her husband in several days.

He'd been murdered. And she had no idea….

* * *

Blake's head was swimming. Should they call Langer first? Tell Mrs. Morris and call in Agent Day? The look on Abby's face showed that she was considering a similar set of anxious thoughts. She'd gone pale when she'd seen the picture, and he was struck by how tired and strained she looked. But really, what else could he have expected? She was still shaking from the visit to Dr. Miles's office. Not to mention the burns on her arms had to be throbbing even with the ibuprofen he'd convinced her to take.

Mrs. Morris, still scavenging through her husband's desk in the alcove behind them, was obliviously content, thinking her dear husband would be home any minute with a million-dollar story. This was the worst part of being a doctor—the moment when you had to tell someone that it was time to give up hope.

"Oh…here. I found something," she said.

Blake pulled his eyes away from Abby and replaced the picture of Morris, aka Hancock, on the side table.

"It's about your family, Dr. Jamison." She scooted out from the desk and returned to the sitting area, handing him a fistful of crumpled papers. "I can't tell if it's old or new."

Blake took the papers, no longer interested in the hospital story against him but only in how to talk to Mrs. Morris about her husband, who wasn't coming back home.

"Would you like a coffee, perhaps? Tea?" she offered. "I always take espresso this time of day. And my boys will be home soon. I'd like to introduce you to Nate, since he used your facility. I think he would like very much to meet you."

"Please," Abby said. "Some coffee would be very nice. Thank you."

Mrs. Morris disappeared around the corner. Abby let out a great sigh.

"What do we say?" she asked.

"I don't know. I guess we should notify Agent Day." Blake handed the papers from Morris's desk to Abby so that he could retrieve his cell phone.

"Or Langer. What if we're wrong?"

"Good point." Blake used his phone and took a picture of the portrait on the side table. He sent the picture to Langer. The accompanying text read:

Lyle Morris, aka Nicolas Hancock?

He looked to Abby for her approval. She nodded. He hit Send. Now they had time to look at the pages that Mrs. Morris had taken from her husband's desk. Abby straightened the papers on her lap and glanced down at the first sheet.

"This is all about you," she said.

They could hear Mrs. Morris making espresso in the next room. The high-pressure machine whistled and dishes clanged. Still, they spoke at a whisper.

"What do you mean it's all about me?" Blake said.

"Here." Abby handed him the first two pages that she'd already looked through.

Blake felt his hands begin to shake as he recognized the documents. "This is a copy of the file from my mother's lawyer. How would Nicolas Hancock, I mean Lyle Morris, get his hands on this?"

"It's about your adoption, isn't it?" Abby handed him the rest of the pages.

Blake nodded. He could feel his pulse racing as he scanned through the rest of the papers from Lyle Morris's desk. "Yes, it's all here. Copies of my mother's letter and the notes from the doctor. This is a copy of the birth record that I found in Lancaster."

"Wow. I guess we know why Hancock was killed. He

was after the same information that you're after. It really is all connected."

"So, Dr. Miles maybe had something to do with my adoption and he was willing to kill to keep it a secret?"

Abby shrugged.

Blake saw his cell phone vibrate on the table. It was a response from Langer. The text read:

Yes. Morris is Hancock. FBI confirmed. Will be there in 20 with FBI agent.

Blake held the cell phone so that Abby could also read the text. Blake typed Okay and reset the phone on the coffee table but the question still remained—should they tell Mrs. Morris the truth before the FBI arrived?

"So, what do we do? Wait?" Abby asked.

There was no chance to respond to her question as Mrs. Morris entered the room holding a large tray with coffee and cookies, which she then placed on the coffee table. Taking the first cup and saucer for Blake, she poured a small espresso for him.

"Would you like sugar?"

"Please." Blake could hardly speak, thinking of what horrible news awaited this poor woman.

She did the same for Abby, then poured a cup for herself and took a seat across from them in a high wing-backed chair.

"We couldn't help but admire all of the photos," Abby said as she sipped her coffee.

"Oh," Mrs. Morris said. "These are just a few of the family, the boys, Lyle and me."

"Is this your husband?" Abby gestured to the photo on the table next to Blake.

"Yes, it was taken just last fall while we were on vacation in the Catskill Mountains. That was just after Nate's surgery. We were celebrating its success. I can't tell you how thankful we are for your foundation, Dr. Jamison."

Blake and Abby both squirmed uncomfortably at her praise.

"Did you find anything interesting in those papers from Lyle's desk?"

"Actually, we did. Somehow your husband has copies of some of my personal and private legal files. I didn't give them to him."

Mrs. Morris's expression darkened. "Are you sure? That doesn't sound like Lyle."

"Yes, I'm sure," Blake said. "In fact, these papers seem to be in high demand. The same ones were stolen last night from my hotel room."

"But that's impossible. Those papers have been here since last week. I'm sure of it. As I told you, my husband hasn't been home. He's working on a story, so these must have already been here before he left."

"Oh, we believe you, Mrs. Morris. We don't think your husband stole the papers from my hotel room. We think he's had them longer than that. Anyway, these are copies. Mine were originals."

"This isn't sounding very good," said Mrs. Morris. "I hope my husband isn't in any trouble. I said earlier that I don't hear from him sometimes when he's working on a story, but usually that's only a day. Maybe two at most. This has been five days."

"I'm afraid we do have bad news."

"The worst kind," Abby said, picking up where he'd left off. "There's an FBI agent and a Lancaster police detective on their way here to talk to you." Blake was just about to tell her about her husband's untimely death when two middle-school-aged boys came busting into the room with their backpacks. They stopped short when they saw that their mother had visitors.

"Bonjour, mes fils." She stood and kissed each of them on the cheek.

"Bonjour, Maman."

"I want to introduce you to Dr. Jamison. He runs the foundation where you had your surgery, Nate."

Blake stood and shook hands with both the boys. He introduced Abby and they passed a few pleasantries. Blake asked many questions about Nate's surgery, all the while feeling like a liar for not telling them about their loss. But at this point, he couldn't imagine telling them—not only that their father had died, but that he'd been murdered. They shouldn't have to hear it from a stranger, and their mother should have a chance to process the news before sharing it with her sons. After a few minutes, Mrs. Morris sent her boys to get a snack in the kitchen and start their homework.

"Have you met my dad?" Nate asked as he was leaving the room. "He's written a lot of articles about you and your foundation."

Blake swallowed down the lump that had formed in his throat. "I haven't had that pleasure."

After the boys had settled away from the living area, Mrs. Morris finished her espresso. Leaning over the coffee table, she spoke in a whisper. "I'm guessing Lyle must be in a lot of trouble if an FBI agent is coming over to the house."

At that moment, there was a knock at the front door. Detective Langer and the FBI agent had arrived. Mrs. Morris looked nervous as she stood and headed for the door. When she returned, she was crying hysterically. She looked up at Blake and Abby. "You already knew, didn't you?"

Blake dropped his head in shame. There was no way he could not feel some of the guilt at the loss of Lyle Morris.

He had no excuses to offer or justifications to share. He simply stammered out a few broken words of condolence, and then he and Abby quietly took their leave.

NINETEEN

Abby and Blake were not allowed to return to Lancaster that night. The FBI put them up at the Waldorf Astoria in a large suite with Detective Langer as their guardian. Abby had never seen anything quite like the hotel as they sat on the fanciest sofa she'd ever seen and had a room-service dinner. Her first ever.

"Your trip to New York was pretty productive," Langer said. "We might never have figured out this ring of adoption scandals if it hadn't been for you two. There may still be some other people involved but the FBI is pretty certain they've got the three main players, Dr. Miles, Mr. Linton and Mr. Pooler."

"But I don't understand," said Abby. "How did it all piece together?"

"Well, first," said Detective Langer, "you recognized Dr. Miles as Hancock's—Morris's—murderer. We caught up with him at the Teterboro Airport in New Jersey. He was getting ready to leave the country after you came to his office and scared him. The FBI is certain after going through his home and office that they will have more than enough incriminating evidence to put him away for murder and kidnapping."

"Okay, I understand the murder charges—he killed

Morris. But kidnapping? Who was kidnapped? Do you mean to tell me that he gave away a baby that wasn't really up for adoption?"

"Exactly," said Blake, who had gotten more of the details out of Langer while Abby had been freshening up. "He stole me and other Amish babies. He would deliver us, then whisk the baby away, apparently telling the family the infant had a terrible disease and needed special treatment. Later, he'd tell them the baby had died and had to be cremated because of risk of infection. He would then sell the baby to rich couples in New York for millions."

"And the lawyers helped make the connections?"

"Right. Linton and Pooler, who are brothers—which explains why I confused them. They all took a cut of the million-dollar adoptions. For thirty years they've been doing this—abusing the most unsuspecting people, the Amish, knowing that they would not be likely to question any doctor's authority."

"No wonder they didn't want anyone to find out about it."

"Where are Pooler and Linton?"

"That we don't know," said Langer. "But we will question Dr. Miles and get more answers over the next few days."

"Well, how did Mr. Morris fit into all of this?" asked Abby. "Why would Pooler give him the files about the adoptions if it incriminated him?"

"Morris knew too much. He had enough information about you and your family to know that you were adopted, and if he dug into it further, he probably discovered that the paperwork wasn't legit. We imagine Pooler tried to bribe him to keep quiet. And when he didn't agree, they—Dr. Miles—decided to eliminate him. Linton called him and convinced him to become a patient at Fairview Hospital under the pretense that he'd be able to access your adoption records. The files Pooler gave him were most likely the bait to convince him of their sincerity. Morris fell for the idea hook, line and sinker. Dr. Miles slipped in and—"

"Shot him full of epinephrine," said Abby. "But why was Blake's name on the hospital file?"

"Well, when you, Dr. Jamison, transferred to Fairview, they all saw embroiling you in the investigation as a way to distract you from looking up the truth, too."

"You mean they were trying to frame me for Hancock's death?"

"Sure. Something to keep you occupied and hopefully get you back to New York."

"And what about Dr. Granger? Granger had to know that I was adopted. Was he in on all of this, too?"

"We don't think so," Langer said. "We think Miles placed his name on the file as another lure to get you back to New York."

"Then why the phony files from Granger?"

"We think Pooler put him up to it as a favor," Langer said. "Which means there may be something else illegal going on over there. We'll look into that another day."

"Eliminate Morris and get Blake back to New York and all would have been fine, except that Miss Miller here cut through the middle of a closed-off wing of the hospital and ruined the whole plan."

"Yes, Abby. If it weren't for you," said Blake, "no one would have known that Hancock was injected. It would have looked like an ordinary cardiac arrest, and I'd have been questioned by the hospital for possible maltreatment of a patient."

"Now, the only question that remains is, who are your real parents?" Abby said.

Langer shook his head. "The FBI thinks that may be a

mystery that's never solved. Between the fire and all the stolen and lost files, the chances of Blake finding his birth parents are not very good." There was a moment of silence as Blake and Abby processed this.

"Well, I think we should all get some rest." Langer stood and waited for Abby and Blake, who didn't move. He blushed, finally realizing that they wanted a moment alone. "After I make a few phone calls. Excuse me."

He slipped into one of the bedrooms.

"I can't believe it." Blake moved in close to her. "It's all over."

Abby shook her head. "I don't know. It still doesn't seem quite finished. If Dr. Miles has been in New York all these years, then how was he able to continue stealing Amish babies? And who grabbed little Stephen in Eli's stable and spoke Pennsylvania Dutch to him?"

"Relax." Blake reached for her hand. "Let the police worry about all that. We're safe for now."

Abby didn't feel safe, but maybe that was because of the man sitting next to her—the one she was falling in love with. She pulled her hand away. Blake Jamison was not for her. "Don't."

"Don't what? Abby, I know you feel this, too. I can see it in your eyes. Don't lie to me and tell me you feel nothing for me."

"This isn't what I want, Blake."

"You don't want...what? Love? A relationship with a man who cares about you? I could take care of you."

"I have to focus on my work. It's the way it has to be."

Blake stood from the sofa and walked away a few feet, turning his back to her. She had hurt him and herself with her words, but he had to know that she was right. They might be attracted to each other, but nothing could ever come of it. They were too different. He knew it as well as she did.

He turned back to her, shaking his head. "Don't you understand? You would never have to work, Abby. Or you could work anywhere you wanted. I could build a clinic for you. Give you everything you ever wanted…"

"I made a promise—"

"To your father?"

"I made a promise to God and to myself. I won't break it. And if you really cared about me, you wouldn't ask me to."

He continued to shake his head as if he couldn't even believe what she was saying to him. "So, you choose work over love?"

"I'm choosing what will give me peace. You should do the same. Good night, Blake. I'm riding back in the morning with Detective Langer. You should stay here in New York. It's where you belong."

Abby got up and ran into her bedroom. She didn't look back as she shut the door behind her. She didn't want Blake to see the tears that might show him what she was really feeling inside.

TWENTY

Abby awoke to the beautiful sounds of birds—larks, bluebirds and robins—singing outside her window. Happy songs of spring and love. It seemed as if the events of the week before had happened years ago. Morris's murder. The car accident. The fire. The trip to New York. Saying goodbye to Blake.

Had that been a mistake?

Abby had struggled all week with her parting words to him. She wished she'd been more honest about her response. She *did* have feelings for him. The fact that she couldn't stop thinking about him was proof of that. But he didn't know what he wanted and he certainly didn't understand what she wanted or needed. He'd come to Lancaster looking for parents, not a romance, and he'd certainly never had any intention of staying. He wasn't a part of her world and she wasn't a part of his.

Yes, she had done the right thing in leaving. Blake would be back in New York permanently now. Dr. Finley had returned early to resume his work in the E.R. Abby could once again concentrate on her clinic and her family. Like today, there was the big wedding at Lydia Yoder's farmhouse. Or rather, soon-to-be Lydia Yoder—today she would marry Joseph Yoder. It was an unusual spring wedding, as most Amish weddings took place in November. The couple had been separated for a long time and requested a special date from the elders of the church.

Her father would be there. He might not like her choices, but today at least he would appreciate that she was wearing an Amish frock and upholding all the traditions that were allowed her under the circumstances.

The smell of roasted coffee brewing rose up to the bedroom from Hannah's kitchen. She'd been staying over at Eli and Hannah's since she'd returned from New York. The FBI had said that the case was wrapping up but she got the impression from Eli—whom she knew had been talking to his police friends behind her back—that it was still not safe for her to go home. But today she was putting all that behind her. She was with family, forgetting the past and moving forward.

"Hey, Abby, are you ready to come on down? There's someone here to see you." Her brother's voice boomed up the narrow stairwell.

Abby hesitated at the bedroom door. It was probably Detective Langer or Chief McClendon, neither of whom she wanted to see. She didn't really want to talk to them any more about the case. She just wanted to move forward.

"I'm coming," she said. "Just a minute."

Why did she feel so nervous? Was it seeing her father again? Abby let out a deep sigh, hoping to expel all her anxiety along with it. Then she prayed a short prayer of thanksgiving and faith for her future. *Oh, Lord, You give me all that is good. And from You I accept whatever You offer me from Your hand.*

Abby knew that all would be well. It just took patience. And then, mentally, spiritually and especially emotionally, it would all make sense again.

Or not...

Abby paused halfway down the stairs. It was not chief McClendon. Nor Detective Langer.

It was Dr. Blake Jamison at the bottom of the stairs. But why? What was he doing back in Willow Trace? Dressed in a suit and tie, he looked as if he planned to go to the wedding, too. His hair was combed back and he wore a grand smile on his face. He had never looked more handsome. Abby walked slowly down the rest of the staircase. She wondered what he thought of her dressed in her traditional *Kapp,* frock and apron.

"You promised me a ride in your buggy. Remember?"

Blake wanted to savor every moment of their buggy ride. He wanted to memorize every detail, from the azure-blue of Abby's frock, complementing her regal eyes, to the ivory creams of her skin, the peach blush of her lips and the golden tendrils of hair, which peeked out from under her pinned-on prayer *Kapp.*

He loved the feel of the buggy, the slow movement of the vehicle rocking back and forth. The steady beat of her gelding Blue-jeans as his hooves clip-clopped across the asphalt matched the even rhythm of Blake's heartbeat. The fresh air he breathed in gave him hope. Part of him wanted to gush out every feeling he had. But his common sense told him that to touch Abby's heart, to fix the damage he'd done, he had to move slowly—slow and steady, like the trot of her brown-and-white horse.

It hadn't taken Blake more than twenty-four hours to realize that he'd said all the wrong things to Abby that night after Dr. Miles had been arrested. He only hoped she hadn't been saying no to *him,* just no to his stupid offers of buying her things and taking her places. That wasn't what Abby wanted. Abby had everything she wanted right here in Lancaster. And so did he, away from the fuss and nonsense of New York that he was more than ready to leave behind. He just hoped that when he moved back here as he planned that she would let him be a part of her life.

"How did you get invited to the Yoder wedding?" She eyed him curiously as she held on to the reins of her horse.

"It's a long story." He smiled, not sure how much to reveal.

"Well, how about the short version?" Her tone told him he still had a ways to go in coaxing her to a softer mood and winning her heart.

"I had to come back to get my things from the bed-and-breakfast. While I was there, the Youngers...well, they convinced me to stay the night. Some of the wedding party was staying at the bed-and-breakfast and they..."

"Invited you to the wedding? Just like that?" Her suspicious look told him she wasn't completely buying his story.

"Hey, you wanted the short version."

"Fair enough."

"I wanted my buggy ride," he said. "And I wanted to see you."

Abby looked away. "Don't. I don't want to go through that again. Let's just enjoy the day."

But I've changed.... The words were silent on his lips. *Everything has changed.* His cell buzzed in his coat pocket, killing his hopeful thoughts. Ugh. He'd forgotten to turn it off. "Sorry. Look. I'm turning it off. Not even looking to see who it is."

He pulled the phone out, turned it off and threw it into the backseat of the buggy.

"That's a smart thing to do," she said. "No one wants a cell phone to go off during a wedding."

"Especially an Amish wedding, right?"

She smiled and, for a second, all felt right with his

world. If only Abby would give him another chance. He would make her see that he did understand her.

"Don't worry. There will be a lot of *Englisch* guests at this wedding. You won't be the only one. Joseph has a lot of *Englisch* clients for his beautiful furniture and I think many of them will be there today."

"So how does it work?"

"You all, the *Englisch,* will be seated on one side, with the Amish men and all the women on the other side."

"Oh, I'm used to bride's side/groom's side."

"If I'd known you were coming," Abby said, "I wouldn't have worn the traditional dress. Then I could have sat with you and explained the ceremony."

While Blake liked the idea of sitting next to Abby at the wedding, he wouldn't have wanted to miss seeing her in the traditional Amish dress. "You've never looked more beautiful. The last week has been so hard."

He tried to take her hand, but she shook her head with an expression of regret.

"Don't. I really just want to enjoy the day. Okay?"

Blake wanted to enjoy the day, too, and in his opinion, holding her hand and talking about the future would make the day quite agreeable. Too bad she didn't feel the same way.

Abby tapped her horse with the reins and Blue-jeans pulled them up a great hill. "This is Holly Hill. It's a beautiful farm. My favorite in all of Willow Trace. Joseph works for my father, who'll be conducting the ceremony."

Abby parked the buggy along with all the others. There was a long, long line of them up and down the hill and many cars, too. She directed Blake toward her brother and off she went with the women. He wondered how long it would be before he'd be able to talk to her again. He already missed her.

The ceremony was brief, only a few words said by her father. Then there was a great meal, more like a feast. The men were seated first in rows and rows of tables and benches lined up in front of the farmhouse. The women served them. Abby was among them. She was busy but he was able to catch her eye a few times. When the meal was over, Blake followed the men to the stable area, where there was much talk and laughter and games. Eli must have read his long expression.

"The women eat inside. They will be out soon." He patted him on the back. "Give her time, Blake. She's a stubborn girl. But she's a smart one, too, and the way she's been moping around here over the last week? Well, I think you two have some things you need to iron out."

"I just hope she'll listen."

It was another hour before the women began to trickle out of the farmhouse kitchen. But Abby was not among them. Blake was starting to lose hope, especially when he saw Hannah bringing a large slice of cake to her husband.

"Is Abigail still inside?" he asked the couple.

Eli looked around, then shrugged. "I suppose she's still helping."

He looked down the long line of buggies. Blake didn't know much about horses but Abby's was a paint, so he was patched with white and brown. He was pretty easy to spot—and he wasn't there.

"Can you ask Hannah? Looks to me like her buggy is gone."

Eli flipped his head toward the line of buggies. "What?"

"Blue-jeans. He was just there between the two chestnuts."

"Yes, he's gone." Eli looked concerned. "The buggy is still there. Someone's unhitched Blue-jeans.... Hannah," he called to his wife, "have you seen Abigail?"

"She was inside a minute ago. Should I go back and look?"

"Yeah, we haven't seen her. And Blue-jeans is missing."

Blake could feel the panic rising through his veins.

Hannah jogged over. "Oh, wait. I remember now. She got a phone call while we were doing dishes."

"A phone call?"

"I assumed she was talking with a patient. That's what it sounded like. But it was noisy in there. You know, all those women talking at the same time."

Blake and Eli exchanged glances.

"She's gone to deliver a baby," Blake said. "I'm sure of it."

"Why wouldn't she tell one of us?" Eli said, his voice a mixture of worry and frustration—the same things Blake was feeling himself.

"I don't have a good feeling about this." Blake turned to Hannah. "Who is close to delivering? Do you know?"

"Francis Cook and…um," Hannah stuttered, "Becka. Becka Esche."

Blake looked at Eli. "Tell me how to get to the Esches' home."

Abby had been helping in the kitchen when her phone buzzed against her hip. While Blake had left his phone in the buggy, she had not. It was too close to Becka's delivery date and she couldn't risk missing her call.

She slipped the phone out of hiding and answered. The other women shot her some disapproving looks, but they would understand soon enough. Still, Hannah raced over, worried that Abby had upset Lydia's mother with her phone call.

"What are you doing?" Hannah said. "Put that away or the ladies are going to kick you out of here for good."

"Becka is due any minute," Abby explained. "I had no choice."

She slipped out the back door of the kitchen. "Hello."

"This is Becka Esche. I know you are at the wedding. But it's time." Becka's voice sounded strange.

"I'll be there as soon as I can. Where is Jonas?"

Becka moaned. "I—I don't know."

"What? You're alone?"

There was a lot of hesitation before Becka answered, "Yes, I'm alone. Hurry, Abigail." Becka cried out as if a labor pain had passed over. At the end of it there was a quick whisper. "Don't come."

"What? Becka, you sound…"

Then the line went dead. Abby paused for a second, anxiety filling her every fiber. *Don't come? Why would Becka say that?* Perhaps she'd meant the baby? Perhaps she was in a lot of pain. It was only natural she'd be scared after losing her first child just after delivery.

After Abigail hung up her cell phone, she raced toward her buggy, berating herself for giving in to Blake's stupid request for a buggy ride. Right now she needed a car.

Abby looked out over the fields surrounding the Stoltz farm. Where were the men? She wanted to tell Blake and Eli where she was going. But she didn't see them anywhere. They were probably all gone to the other side of the barn to play a game. In any case, there was no time for her to waste searching. Blake would only want to come with her, which Becka and Jonas wouldn't want. She wasn't too sure she did, either. In any case, Hannah knew what had happened. She'd been standing there when the cell phone rang along with ten other women who all knew Becka Esche was about to deliver. Any one of those women could tell the boys what had happened and they would figure out where she was…if they even noticed she was gone.

Abby arrived at her buggy and chucked her cell phone into the front seat. Becka's panicked voice rang through her ears. The buggy might be too slow, she thought. So Abby unhitched Blue-jeans. She would ride him to the Esches'. Cutting across the Lapps' and the Youngers' fields, she would be there in no time.

"I don't like this," said Blake.

"How long ago did she receive that phone call?" Eli asked his wife.

"A while." Hannah shrugged and Blake realized she had no watch. Whatever figure she came up with would be pure conjecture.

"Like 'twenty minutes' a while or like 'over an hour'?" Eli placed a hand on Hannah's shoulder. "I didn't tell you this because I didn't want you to worry. But the FBI is still looking for Anthony Linton and Pooler."

"What?" Hannah's expression darkened. "Why didn't you tell me? Abigail is still in danger, isn't she?"

"I didn't know this, either," Blake said.

"You were in New York," Eli explained. "The FBI had you under surveillance. They didn't want you or Abby to know because they want Linton and Pooler to think it's safe to come out."

"Then someone is watching Abby now?"

"I don't know. At first, they were certain that Linton had left the country with Pooler. But now they aren't so sure. There are phone calls back to someone in the States. So they think Linton or someone is still here. In Lancaster."

"Linton?"

"I guess."

"I have a really bad feeling about Abby's taking off like this." Blake's pulse was already rising when he followed

Eli's pointed finger, which directed everyone's eyes across the grassy field to an approaching white truck.

"That's Chief McClendon," said Eli.

"And he's headed right for us." Blake shook his head. Abby was in trouble. He could feel it.

"I hate to interrupt the wedding—" McClendon spoke quickly "—but there didn't seem to be any other way to get in touch with you."

Blake felt his pockets before remembering he'd left his cell phone in the buggy. "Why? What's happened?"

"More like what's happening." McClendon looked through the wedding guests. "Where is Abigail? She needs to hear this, too."

"We aren't sure," said Blake. "It seems she went to deliver a baby without telling anyone. On horseback. I doubt she has her phone."

McClendon frowned and swallowed hard. Blake did not like the look on the chief's face.

"What is it?" he asked. "Why did you come to the wedding?"

"The FBI found Pooler and Linton. They were both on Grand Cayman. But Dr. Dodd was not with them."

"Dr. Dodd? What's he got to do with anything?" Blake said, thinking about the overly efficient administrator of Fairview.

"Everything. He has everything to do with this—he was the brains behind the whole concept. He started the whole affair of stealing and selling Amish babies and has continued it for over thirty years. He's a very dangerous man and the FBI thinks he's still inside of Lancaster County. He was brought up Amish, so he knows how to blend in, play the part, disappear and fool others."

"Wow. That explains a lot. And where better to hide in Lancaster County than among the Amish?" said Eli.

"Come on. Let's go find Abigail and hunt down this baby-stealing monster."

Blake was already halfway to Chief McClendon's truck, where he saw Detective Langer already seated at the wheel.

"Where are we going?" said McClendon.

"To Becka Esche's."

Abby was really sorry that she wasn't wearing a pair of pants. Blue-jeans was a great horse to ride, but not bare-back and not in her Amish frock. She hadn't done this since she and Hannah were little girls. And just like back then, her prayer *Kapp* dropped to the ground and her hair danced around her shoulders with the beat of the horse's gait. But after she got over the initial discomfort, muscle memory kicked in. So, once the gelding settled into a steady canter, Abby was able to join the horse's rhythm and think about what lay ahead.

Becka had gained very little weight during her pregnancy. What little bit she had eaten never seemed to stay down. Abby had never felt that Becka's pregnancy had been healthy and she had begged her—as she did all her patients—to see a licensed gynecologist at least once. But Becka and her husband, Jonas, had refused. With most of her Amish patients, the idea of a gynecologist did not sit well and was considered an unnecessary modern practice. But that was not the whole story with Jonas and Becka. They had actually been to the hospital with their first pregnancy. The baby had been born with a rare disease and died within hours of delivery. After that, nothing would convince either of them to return to a hospital or an *Englisch* doctor. And Abby could hardly blame them after such a bad experience. In fact, she thought it quite possible that stress and anxiety were the reasons for Becka's difficult pregnancy.

Thinking of Jonas, it was odd he wasn't at home with Becka. Jonas knew Becka was near term, and after what had happened last time, what could possibly have kept him from his wife? Abby could not imagine. As she rode up on their little cottage, she looked around. The place seemed eerily quiet. No dogs? No Jonas waiting at the door for her?

"Jonas?"

Abby saw their buggies parked by the paddock. Their three horses grazed in a small field next to the house. Abby dismounted, pulled off the bit and reins, and steered Blue-jeans into the field with the other horses. Jonas must be inside with Becka, she thought. He couldn't be far. All of his horses were there and Jonas was a carpenter. He and Becka didn't have a big farm or lots of animals to tend to over a big spread of land. Even from the farthest edge of their property, he should have heard her approaching. So why hadn't he come up to the door to greet her and take her horse?

The muscles in her neck tensed. Something wasn't right. She moved faster toward the house.

"Becka? Jonas?"

A woman's cry of pain pierced the still air. It was Becka. Was the baby already coming?

Please, Lord, please, let Becka and the baby be healthy.

Almost running now, Abby entered the house. Becka was on her back on the hardwood floor, a blanket thrown over her legs and lap. Her lips and face were gray with pain. Jonas stroked her hair. His eyes were closed as he whispered up prayers in a rotelike fashion.

Becka opened her tearstained eyes and tried to focus on Abby. "I told you not to come."

Abby stopped fast as she understood why Becka was on the floor, why Jonas was praying, why Becka had told her not to come.

Across the room, seated in a comfortable upholstered chair, was Dr. Dodd. He had a large handgun aimed at the Esche couple and a big creepy smile for her.

"We've been waiting for you," he said. A disgusting snarl slid across his face and he laughed. "You, Miss Miller, are going to deliver your last baby. But not here."

He stood, waving his gun around, as he walked toward the couple, holding the gun over Becka's head. "Pick her up and put her in the car," he ordered Jonas.

"What?" Abby knew why he wanted them to move. He knew as well as she did that others would join them soon. That didn't make the idea any less insane. "You can't move her in this condition. You're a doctor. You know this. Look at her. She's in agony and in labor."

"Of course she's in labor. I gave her a huge dose of Pitocin, too. Should speed things up. I don't have a whole lot of time. I need that baby."

"I have no idea what you're talking about," Abby said. "But you will be putting the baby and the mother at risk if you move them."

"I'm holding a gun. You are all at risk." He laughed.

Good point. Abby sighed. She was not going to win this fight, but she would do whatever she had to do to keep Becka and her baby alive.

Jonas didn't wait any longer. He scooped his struggling wife into his arms and stood.

"You." Dodd pointed the gun at Abby. "You're driving. My car is around back. I think you'll recognize it."

Abby glanced out the back door, which was wide open. Parked behind the house was the same black sedan that had run her off the road last week. One by one, they filed out of the house and into the car. Dodd pointed his gun at one head and then at another, reminding them that obeying was their only option if they wanted to stay alive—for now.

* * *

"There's Blue-jeans!" Blake saw Abby's horse, happily grazing in the small paddock next to the tiny home that Eli had directed them to. Fortunately, it was not too far from the Holly Hill Farmhouse. But still, they had no idea how much time had passed since Abby had arrived. Blake shivered. Abby could have fallen into Dodd's hands over an hour ago.

Langer parked the Lancaster County Police truck in front of the house. Blake and Eli leaped from the vehicle.

"You go inside." Eli ran as he spoke, holding the spare handgun he'd taken from McClendon. He let his black felt hat fall to the ground behind him. "I'm going to cover the perimeter. Make sure no one goes anywhere."

McClendon and Langer radioed in their location and followed close behind.

Blake flew through the front door and into the tiny living space. He stopped short over a pool of blood covering a small area in the center of the hardwood floor. A white-and-yellow quilt had been thrown to the side. It was also stained with fresh blood. The rest of the house was as neat as a pin but empty. Completely empty.

"They're not here." Blake exited the Esches' home through the open back door, meeting up with Eli, who'd just circled around the outside. "But there is blood on the floor. If that's Becka's blood then there could be complications, unless she's already delivered."

"She didn't deliver yet. Dodd wants her baby. If the labor was over, he and the child would be gone and everyone else would be here."

"He moved a woman in labor?"

"Probably at gunpoint. I don't see Abby going along with it any other way."

"You're right."

"Tire marks right here." Eli pointed at the muddy ground. "These are fresh. It rained during the night. If they're in a car, they could be anywhere. It could take days to find them. If he lets them live…"

Days? Lets them live? More panic washed over Blake. He shook his head, clearing his thoughts. "Abby told me about Becka's pregnancy—that she had problems last time delivering the placenta. Maybe Abby convinced everyone to go to the hospital?"

McClendon and Detective Langer caught up with them after combing through the house behind Blake. "Unlikely. Eli's right. They are going to be hard to find."

Blake couldn't accept that. "Dodd wants that baby. He won't risk sabotaging the delivery. I don't think he'll go far."

"I'll send units to the hospital," McClendon said. "But that sounds risky for Dodd. Too many people—people who would recognize him."

Blake thought hard. Where else could they go with proper medical facilities for the delivery? Somewhere close-by… "Abby's clinic?"

McClendon looked to Eli. Eli nodded. "Certainly worth a look."

The four men raced back to McClendon's police car and headed toward Abby's cottage, hoping they had guessed correctly and praying that they wouldn't arrive too late.

Jonas helped Abby place his wife on the examination table of her clinic.

"The same London family wants a sibling," said Dodd. "I've already chartered a flight to London for this afternoon."

"The same family?" Abby's brain took a second but then the whole affair made sense to her. "Becka's first baby didn't die, did it? You stole it and sold it. And now you want this one, too."

Thankfully, Dodd was so obsessed with getting the Esches' child she'd been able to convince him that he'd have the infant in less than ten minutes and that she'd needed a decent delivery setting immediately. She'd been bluffing, of course. She hadn't even examined her patient. She'd had no idea how long it would take. But now that they were in her clinic, she realized that she had not been far from the truth. Becka's baby was well on its way. Abby cleaned herself up and began coaching Becka through the labor. Jonas helped, too, making Becka as comfortable as possible.

It didn't take long—not even ten minutes. But for those very few minutes, Abby had been able to forget about the gun pointed at the back of her head and concentrate on the miracle of birth, on the comfort of her patient and on the safe delivery of the Esches' child.

"It's a girl." She delivered the infant into the arms of her father, then cut the umbilical cord. Jonas was crying. Becka looked gray and in more pain than Abby thought she had ever seen in any mother. She didn't seem to even understand that the baby had come.

"She's healthy," Abby told Becka. "Everything is going to be fine."

And that was what Abby had thought until the second she cut the cord. It retracted.

That wasn't supposed to happen.

Becka tucked up into a ball, hardly able to endure the pain. It was happening again. Her placenta was still attached. Just like last time when they'd been in the hospital and Dodd had stolen their first baby. At least then another doctor had been there to take the necessary measures to save Becka. Dodd was her only hope. Delivering an attached placenta was tricky, dangerous and if not done correctly could cause infection and death.

"Dr. Dodd, you have to help her. Her placenta is attached." Abby turned to the crazed doctor.

"I don't have to do anything." Dodd moved forward. He shoved Abby to the ground and put a bullet through her stomach. "Like I said. This was your last delivery."

Abby fell back to the floor. She grabbed at her midsection. Gritting her teeth, she pressed down on the hole before it had even begun to bleed. She could do nothing but watch as Dodd grabbed the baby from Jonas's arms.

He was too focused on the infant to even notice that his carelessly aimed shot hadn't hit any vital organs. There was still a chance that blood loss could finish her, but if she was able to get treatment in time, she'd survive. She was careful not to draw his attention in her direction, or he might notice. If he fired a second, more fatal shot, she wouldn't be able to help Becka.

"I don't have to worry about you. You won't fight back," he said to Jonas and then he was gone. Abby could hear the tires of his car crunching over the gravel as he sped out of her driveway, taking the Esches' child with him.

Abby closed her eyes as the pain receptors from her abdomen reached her brain and told it she'd been shot.

Please, Lord, she prayed, *please. I need Your hands and Your strength.*

Somehow, she was going to get up off that floor and she was going to do whatever she could to save Becka Esche. And she was going to pray that the FBI was right behind Dodd on its way to recover the Esche baby—and that the paramedics would make it to her clinic soon, for Becka's sake...and for her own.

"I don't see anyone there." Blake's heart sank to his stomach as McClendon's squad car pulled up in front of Abby's cottage and clinic.

"No, look!" Eli put a hand on his shoulder. "The front door is open. Someone has been here."

Detective Langer drew his pistol and led the way into Abby's house. Blake and Eli followed close behind. None of them were prepared for what they saw as they entered the clinic.

"He's gone." Abby's voice was weak as she sat next to her patient holding a set of delivery forceps. "He took the baby with him. You have to find him."

"You've been hurt!" Blake rushed forward, only half hearing Abby's words. He pulled her hand away from her waist. "You've been shot."

"Forget...that. I'm...fine." She turned his attention toward Becka Esche as she struggled to breathe and speak. "She needs...help. The afterbirth..."

"Please, you're a doctor, aren't you?" An Amish-dressed man stood next to Abby's patient. He was so calm and quiet Blake had hardly noticed him there. He must be Mr. Esche. "I've been praying that you would come and save my Becka."

Blake's head swirled. He looked back at Abby, hesitating. She'd been shot. She was bleeding and hadn't stopped to bandage the wound. Already she had lost a lot of blood as she'd clearly been trying to use every bit of her energy to save her patient.

She wasn't fine.

Every bit of Blake's will told him to check Abby and her wound. To save her, to save the woman he'd come back to Lancaster for. The woman he loved and he didn't want to live without.

She shook her head at him. "I can wait for the EMTs. She can't. She's already passed out."

Abby held out the forceps for him. Blake resigned himself to doing what Abby wanted.

He turned to the sink. "I need to scrub. Eli, you'll assist me. For starters, wash your hands. Grab that brown bottle over there and those strips of bandages."

With dripping but clean hands, Blake returned to the exam table. He took the instrument from Abby. "Pour that over the ends," he said to Eli, nodding to the bottle of povidone-iodine, a topical antiseptic, that he held.

Eli did as he said, sterilizing the tool that he would try to save Becka Esche with.

"Now, pour that same stuff all over the front and back of your sister's wound and wrap it up as tightly as possible. I'm assuming Langer has already called the EMS?" Blake knew his voice sounded detached and unfeeling, when it was the furthest thing from the truth. Inside he was dying with a panic that he'd never felt before in his whole career—his whole life.

Eli did exactly what he was told. Abby moaned as he pulled the bandages tight around her abdomen. It seemed like forever before the EMS arrived. Forever, while he struggled to save Becka and watched Abby grow paler by the minute.

But EMS arrived at last and they swept away both Becka and Abby and raced off to Fairview without him. Now all he could do was wait and pray....

TWENTY-ONE

Abby had been in surgery for what seemed like hours to Blake. He waited outside the operatory. He sat. He stood. He paced. Abby's father sat next to him. Her mother, too. And Eli and Hannah.

"How's that search for your birth parents going?" Bishop Miller asked.

Blake shook his head. "The FBI said it was a lost cause. That they'll never be able to track down all the families Dodd stole babies from."

Anyway, he didn't care about that. All he cared about was Abby.

"You care for my daughter, don't you?" Bishop Miller asked.

"I love her."

The bishop nodded his head. Other than that, there seemed to be no reaction to Blake's confession.

"Maybe you should know I plan to move here and hopefully court your daughter...I mean, if she'll agree to that."

Again, the bishop just nodded. "I've made my peace with it, son. Relax."

Eli had been on his cell. He tucked it away and walked over to them. "They found the Esches' baby and arrested Dodd."

Blake felt a fraction of the tension inside him relax. At least the monster who had shot Abby would face charges for his crimes. "And how is Becka?"

"She's fine."

"Has she seen her baby?"

"Not yet," said Hannah. "She's in the NICU."

Everyone sat again as there wasn't much else to say, and they waited. At long last, the E.R. surgeon came out.

"We removed the bullet. Luckily, it managed to avoid any major organs. Due to the blood loss, she'll be here for a few more days. But she will make a full recovery. She can have visitors, too—one at a time."

Abby's father headed toward Recovery without looking back.

"Wait, *Dat*. Let Blake go first," Eli said.

"No." Blake smiled. "She will want to see her dad first."

He didn't know if that was true or not but he wanted the bishop to be satisfied, and now that he knew she was going to be fine, he could stand to wait another five minutes. Blake was so happy and so nervous about what he had to tell Abby or ask Abby—a few minutes more to gather his thoughts might be a good thing.

Abby was surprised to see her father as her first visitor.

"How are you feeling, Abigail?" Her father sat next to her bedside and patted her hand.

"I've been better." She started to laugh. "Oooh. That hurts."

"You just rest. I'll do the talking," her *dat* said. "There's a line of people waiting to get in here to see you. So, I'll make it quick."

Abby wondered if Blake was one of those people. She thought she had seen him come into her clinic. She vaguely remembered handing him the forceps to help Becka. Then again, maybe it had all been a dream.

"*Dat,* if you're here to tell me I made the wrong decision again, then please don't."

"I just told you that I was going to do the talking. Be quiet and listen. Goodness, you're as stubborn as your *mamm.*" He cleared his throat and patted her hand again. "I didn't come here to talk to you about your decision. Well, I did. But…"

Abby held her breath—she did not want to hear her father's disapproval once more.

"I came to tell you that I've been wrong," he said. "I wanted you to join the church. I wanted you to marry an Amish man. I wanted you to give me lots of grandbabies and be a farmer's wife. Or a carpenter's wife. Or a miller's wife… So, I let you go to school. I let you go to college. I let you work at the hospital. I let you start the clinic, thinking all the time that any day you would get tired of the outside world and all the complications. That you would give it up and come back home. And then I realized that home is where each one of us finds peace with the Lord. And you have that. All this time, Abby, you are home. You have been home. I just couldn't see it."

Abby could feel the tears pouring down her cheeks as she watched her dad touch his heart with his hand. "You are home. You were meant to be a nurse. And I'm very proud of you."

"Thank you, *Dat.* Thank you for understanding. I love you so much."

"And I love you, too. And now I have some things to do and you have other people to see. Get some rest and get better." He kissed her forehead and turned and left the room.

Moments later, Blake entered Abby's room and approached her slowly. She couldn't blame him for being cautious after all the pushing away she'd done. She was surprised he was brave enough to come in.

"I hope those are happy tears?" he said.

"The happiest." She smiled. "You saved Becka. Thank you."

"*You* saved Becka. I just came in and helped her hang on until the EMS arrived."

He reached her bedside. She motioned for him to sit down where her father had been. "They found Dodd and the baby. She's fine. She's here and ready to meet you. In the latest news from Hannah just a minute ago, I heard that her name is going to be Abigail."

"Stop," Abby said. "I'm going to start crying again and it hurts."

"Okay. I'll stop. In any case, I really wanted to talk about something else."

Abby didn't want to hear again about how he was leaving and going back to New York. The past week had been bad enough. She didn't want to live it all over again. "Do we have to talk, Blake? I'm scared. I can't be what you need. Just hold my hand and be my friend while you're here. I know that's all we can have."

"Shh. I'm going to talk, Abby. And you? You're just going to have to listen to me. No interrupting. Okay?"

"Have you been talking to my *dat?*"

He ignored her comment and resumed his speech, which sounded a bit as if he'd rehearsed it. "I know I haven't known you very long. I know I haven't been in Lancaster very long. But I know what right is, Abby. I know what peace of mind is. And I know what home feels like. This is my home. Not New York. Not the private practice. Not the big apartment and the cover stories. *Right* is my being here. That's home for me—being with you. It's what I want and it's where I'm going to be."

"What?" Was she dreaming? Was she hearing him correctly? "What about your practice? Your foundations? Natalie? New York?"

"My partners are buying me out. I'm going to work here at Fairview. Natalie is engaged to Artie. Remember Artie? And I've taken up a permanent room at the bed-and-breakfast. You can't get rid of me. I'm here to stay. I love it here. And I love you."

"What about the foundation? What about finding your birth parents?" *Did he just say that he loves me?*

"I'm moving the foundation to Lancaster. And I gave up finding my birth parents. I thought I was coming here for that and I guess that is what brought me. But that wasn't what I was looking for, Abby. I was looking for you. I just didn't know it."

Abby felt frozen in the wonderful dream. She'd just had a bullet removed but she couldn't feel any pain. There was nothing but happiness inside.

"Abby? Did you hear me? I'm falling in love with you." He leaned over and kissed her softly on the lips.

"Oh, I hear you, Blake. I hear you." More happy tears fell from her eyes. "Kiss me again."

"I would…but I have something I need to know first," he teased her.

"Fair enough."

"I heard you were never going to consider marriage. Ever. Is that true? Or is that up for negotiation? Because that might make a difference in how I kiss you…"

Abby felt the smile burst over her face. This was it. This was the man she was going to spend the rest of her life with. As a nurse, helping others and being so in love she thought she would burst.

"Are doctors allowed to marry their patients?" She lifted her eyes playfully.

Blake smiled. He knew her answer. "Well, this doctor plans to marry his patient—his one very stubborn, Amish-born, beautiful, wonderful, favorite patient. What do you say, Abigail Miller? Marry me?"

"Yes, Blake. I'll marry you. I love you so much."

He leaned in again and sealed her answer with another kiss.

* * * * *

Dear Reader,

Thank you so much for reading *Lancaster County Target*. I hope you enjoyed Blake and Abby's adventure. Since Abby Miller has made appearances in two other stories, it seemed appropriate for her to star in her own romantic suspense. I always love adding a little twist to a tried-and-true story line like a doctor-nurse romance. My favorite part is giving the characters their happy ending. It was exciting, too, to have Eli and Hannah from *Plain Secrets* and Lydia and Joseph from *Return to Willow Trace* appear in this story—all part of the fun for me in writing a series.

This was an interesting story, too, in that while the Amish community evokes one type of mood for readers, hospitals can stir up all sorts of emotions for us depending on our own experiences. In this story, I wrote about placenta accreta, which one of my friends had a scary experience with. It also brought back some reflections of my own hospital experience, which you can read about in my blog archives. All I want to say here is that I hold some doctors and nurses in very high esteem. What they do is not easy. The patients are not always pleasant or grateful. And sometimes things happen so quickly that everyone is just praying it's the correct treatment or diagnosis. They are true-life heroes in my book.

As always, I love to hear from readers. I would love to know your thoughts on *Lancaster County Target*. Please visit with me at www.kitwilkinson.com. You can email me at write@kitwilkinson.com or address a letter to Love Inspired Books, 233 Broadway, Suite 1001, New York, New York 10279.

Many blessings,
Kit Wilkinson

Questions for Discussion

1. Blake goes to Lancaster to search for his birth parents, but he ends up finding family in a different way. Have you ever set out on a journey that took you somewhere unexpected? Discuss yours and Blake's experiences.

2. Discuss the pros and cons of adoption. When is it appropriate to tell a child that he/she is adopted, or is it not appropriate to tell them at all? Have you ever thought of adopting a child?

3. Would you want to know if you were adopted? Why or why not? Would you search for your birth parents?

4. Discuss Abby's struggle to break away from her culture and especially her father. Have you ever been torn between two paths? How did you choose what to do? Do you think Abby would have been happy if she had joined the Amish church?

5. Discuss Blake Jamison. Is he an easy hero to like at all times? Why or why not?

6. Discuss the role of Abby's father in the story. If you have children, what are your expectations for them? How do you deal with it when they choose something other than what you think is best? What moments are hardest for parents and why?

7. What is your favorite scene in the novel and why?

8. 1 Chronicles 28:9 says, "Acknowledge the God of your father, and serve him with wholehearted devotion and

with a willing mind, for the Lord searches every heart and understands every desire and every thought. If you seek him, he will be found by you; but if you forsake him, he will reject you forever." How does this verse apply to Abby's and Blake's stories?

9. Illegal adoptions take place more frequently than you might think. What precautions should couples take to avoid these situations and the people orchestrating them, who often take a couple's money and never actually deliver a baby? What can the government do to prevent this, if anything?

10. Discuss the Amish dilemma of using or not using modern medicine and/or modern technology during a pregnancy or other complicated medical condition. Do you appreciate their standpoint? How do you view this part of the Amish culture?

11. In this story, I mention chicken potpie and Church Soup—the recipes can be found on my website. What are some of your favorite Amish dishes? If you have never tried Amish food, are there any dishes that you would like to try? Why or why not?

12. In the beginning of the novel, Abby feels as if Blake is hiding who he really is from her. Discuss how that is partially true and how the reverse is also true— that she is also very guarded around him and others. Why might they both have a tendency to be guarded?

13. Romans 12:2 says, "Do not conform to the pattern of this world, but be transformed by the renewing of your mind. Then you will be able to test and approve what

God's will is—his good, pleasing and perfect will."
Discuss how this verse applies to the Amish culture
versus mainstream American Christian lifestyles. Do
you think Abby made the right choice by leaving the
Amish faith? Why or why not?

REQUEST YOUR FREE BOOKS!

2 FREE RIVETING INSPIRATIONAL NOVELS
PLUS 2 FREE MYSTERY GIFTS

YES! Please send me 2 FREE Love Inspired® Suspense novels and my 2 FREE mystery gifts (gifts are worth about $10). After receiving them, if I don't wish to receive any more books, I can return the shipping statement marked "cancel." If I don't cancel, I will receive 4 brand-new novels every month and be billed just $4.74 per book in the U.S. or $5.24 per book in Canada. That's a savings of at least 21% off the cover price. It's quite a bargain! Shipping and handling is just 50¢ per book in the U.S. and 75¢ per book in Canada.* I understand that accepting the 2 free books and gifts places me under no obligation to buy anything. I can always return a shipment and cancel at any time. Even if I never buy another book, the two free books and gifts are mine to keep forever.

123/323 IDN F5AC

Name	(PLEASE PRINT)

Address	Apt. #

City	State/Prov.	Zip/Postal Code

Signature (if under 18, a parent or guardian must sign)

Mail to the Harlequin® Reader Service:
IN U.S.A.: P.O. Box 1867, Buffalo, NY 14240-1867
IN CANADA: P.O. Box 609, Fort Erie, Ontario L2A 5X3

**Are you a current subscriber to Love Inspired Suspense books
and want to receive the larger-print edition?
Call 1-800-873-8635 or visit www.ReaderService.com.**

* Terms and prices subject to change without notice. Prices do not include applicable taxes. Sales tax applicable in N.Y. Canadian residents will be charged applicable taxes. Offer not valid in Quebec. This offer is limited to one order per household. Not valid for current subscribers to Love Inspired Suspense books. All orders subject to credit approval. Credit or debit balances in a customer's account(s) may be offset by any other outstanding balance owed by or to the customer. Please allow 4 to 6 weeks for delivery. Offer available while quantities last.

Your Privacy—The Harlequin® Reader Service is committed to protecting your privacy. Our Privacy Policy is available online at www.ReaderService.com or upon request from the Harlequin Reader Service.
We make a portion of our mailing list available to reputable third parties that offer products we believe may interest you. If you prefer that we not exchange your name with third parties, or if you wish to clarify or modify your communication preferences, please visit us at www.ReaderService.com/consumerschoice or write to us at Harlequin Reader Service Preference Service, P.O. Box 9062, Buffalo, NY 14269. Include your complete name and address.

LIS13R

Can an estranged couple find a way to mend fences when they're forced into Witness Protection together?

Read on for a preview of FAMILY IN HIDING by Valerie Hansen, part of the WITNESS PROTECTION series from Love Inspired Suspense.

Grace parked in the shade across from the school and released her three-year-old from his booster seat and looked for her two children.

It wasn't hard to spot her eldest. His red hair stood out like a lit traffic flare at an accident scene when he left the main building and started in her direction. Then he paused, pivoted and ran right up to a total stranger.

The man crouched to embrace the boy, setting Grace's nerves on edge and causing her to react immediately.

"Hey! What do you think you're doing?"

The figure stood in response to her challenge. The brim of a cap and dark glasses masked his eyes, yet there was something very familiar about the way he moved.

Grace gaped. It couldn't be. But it was. "Dylan?"

He placed a finger against his lips. "Shush. Not here. We need to talk."

When he removed the glasses, Grace was startled to glimpse an unusual gleam in her estranged husband's eyes, as if he might be holding back tears—which, of course, was out of the question, knowing him.

"If you want to speak to me you can do it through my lawyer, the way we agreed."

"This has nothing to do with our divorce. It's much more important than that."

Grace's first reaction was disappointment, followed rapidly by resentment. "What can possibly be more important than our marriage and the future of our children?"

"I'm beginning to realize that my priorities need adjustment, but that's not why we have to talk. In private."

"What could you possibly have to say to me that can't be said right here?"

"Let me put it this way, Grace," Dylan said quietly, cupping her elbow and leaning closer. "You can either come with me and listen to what I have to say, or get ready to save a bunch of money, because you won't have to pay your divorce attorney."

"Why on earth not?"

Dylan scanned the crowd and clenched his jaw before he said, "Because you'll probably be a widow."

*Will Grace and Dylan find a way to save
their marriage and their lives?
Pick up FAMILY IN HIDING to find out.
Available May 2014 wherever
Love Inspired® Suspense books are sold.*

Love Inspired®
SUSPENSE
RIVETING INSPIRATIONAL ROMANCE

GUARDIANS, INC.

Bodyguards Chloe Howard and T. J. Davenport are no strangers to danger. But when they're assigned to safeguard a controversial couple on a book tour through Texas, the biggest danger is each other. Nine years ago they worked a case, fell in love...and walked away, leaving Chloe with a broken heart. But reuniting with her strong, fearless ex makes her remember desires best forgotten. Now, as a determined killer closes in, with them and their clients in his sights, Chloe knows there's only one way to stay alive: fight the attraction. Because for a bodyguard, the greatest danger is falling in love....

BODYGUARD REUNION
by
MARGARET DALEY

*Available April 2014 wherever Love Inspired
books and ebooks are sold.*

LIS44595